Gathering Moss

OTHER BOOKS BY KAMRYN ADAMS

Par for the Curse

When the Butterfly Falls

Stay in Your Lane

AUTHORS NOTE

Gathering Moss

By

Kamryn Adams

IMPRESA BOOKS

Published by Impresa Books

Impresa Books
The Kamryn Adams Group

10 9 8 7 6 5 4 3 2 1

Publishers Note
This is a work of fiction. All events and characters in this story are solely the product of the author's imagination. Any similarities between any characters and situations presented in this book to any individuals, living or dead, or actual places and situation are purely coincidental.

ISBN: 9780990871323 (Paperback)
Printed in the United States of America

For My Soror, Nikki May

Thank you for pushing me to finish the story of these girls.

Thank you for loving them enough to keep them alive.

Skee-Wee!

PROLOGUE

Growing up under the cast iron opinion and leather belts of my Aunt Janice, I only wanted one thing — a real family. So I did what I had to do to get one. In college, I found the hottest guy on campus and made sure he fell deeply, head over heels in love with me. They say once you go Black you never go back. That was certainly the case for my husband, Greg.

Greg got a taste of chocolate and he was hooked. Though his mother nearly had a fit, he was hell bent on marrying me — a smart, pretty cocoa brown girl with no parents, no siblings, seemingly nothing to offer his rich blue-blood family heritage. It was bad enough that his best friend from childhood was Black, but marrying a Black woman sent his mother to the edge. Too bad she did not fall off of it. Eva Goodwyn never liked me and quite frankly I never cared for her much either.

She knew I was not necessarily in love with her son but more in love with the concept of the life that he could give me. Eva recognized that trait in me because she herself was South Jersey white trash that married out of her social class.

She was reaping what she had sown as a trampy, scheming young racist. It was only fitting that her precious son would fall in love with a scheming, tramping young black girl.

It was nothing personal toward Greg. In fact, I respect my husband tremendously. He's the best thing a woman could ask for in a husband. He's smart, sexy, kind, and a hell of a provider. Most women would feel very lucky to have Greg as their life-long mate. Unfortunately for him I am not most women.

As a young girl I never cared much for boys. They annoyed me. As I got older, I saw the opposite sex as two things: a distraction from my goal to become a psychiatrist and a way to resource my plan to do such. I'm not a latent homosexual. I am just not an overly enthusiastic heterosexual.

Greg was a hottie. He came from good family stock and he gave me an entree into a new world of old money. My Aunt Janice was so very pleased with my choice. She raised me to find a man just like Greg…smart, rich, and "he better be white," she said. Aunt Janice was not fond of Black men.

Since I had no family to love me when I was growing up, I never learned to love anyone else. I never had so much as a stuffed animal to bond with during my early childhood and that made it difficult for me. Then my girl, Callista Piper, moved next door. She was an orphan like me, kind of.

My best friend, "Callie" is as white as white girls come… rather thin but with curves, bright blonde hair, with deep blue eyes that made women of all races envious. The Black family next door to Aunt Janice and me adopted her. We became fast friends. "Fast" being the optimal word. When it came to boys, Callie taught me how to give head and give 'em hell. It was no wonder she became a police officer and quickly promoted to detective. She was the baddest, strongest, realist woman I knew. She completely shatters the stereotype of white women being fragile and weak.

Callie was the Maid of Honor in my wedding. For that reason, she has not always supported my "extra-curricular" activities. But, she still loved me anyway. She was the first real, still living family member I had. Aunt Janice was alive, but she was so fake that she belonged at Madame Tussaud's wax museum. She most definitely did not fit my description of "family."

Greg and I were married sixteen years before my life came crumbling to pieces along with my sobriety. I had everything I wanted and a bunch of stuff I never even thought I would need. My museum-sized home was more than enough for my husband, my daughter and me. I had the wealthiest and most handsome husband in the neighborhood. We were the kind of family that you see on cereal commercials. We looked the part.

Greg, Bryann and I looked perfect on the outside but our lives were a mess, individually and collectively as a unit. I suppose we were always a disaster waiting to happen but I just thought we would escape it. My daughter's bipolar mania made life very challenging at times. If she was not on her medication she could be a handful to manage; smoking marijuana, impulse shopping, and having sex with random boys.

This was unthinkable for Greg, who wished to control every aspect of our daughter's life the way his mother had controlled his up until he met me. He had Bryann's entire life planned out before she was even a month old — college, career, and activities. She was to be a dancer, a ballerina. Her mental illness and complete lack of interest in anything other than reading and writing poetry crushed his dreams of that.

Greg was the ultimate stoic. The word fun, though clearly three letters, was a four-letter word to my husband. His favorite pastime was making money. To Greg, showing emotion was a sign of weakness unless, of course, it was in response to some serious capital gains in the market. As for me, well… I'm a recovering alcoholic who recently ended ten years of sobriety thanks to my girlfriend Olive Jones, whom I call "Liv" and her willingness to let me toss one back. One became two and two became hidden bottles of vodka under the kitchen sink.

Liv meant well. If ever there was a time for her to offer me a drink it was certainly the day Riley Briggs and Kane Taylor walked into my life. Kane, my lover, is Riley's cousin. Of course, he hid that from me until he was under oath on the witness stand. I finally fell in love with someone and he turned out to be a total fraud. It was all a set up for Riley to destroy my marriage and get visitation rights to my daughter — to whom she gave birth.

You see, my daughter was adopted and until Riley Briggs showed up Bryann never knew that well hidden fact. Bryann tried to kill herself when she found out that Greg and I had kept this secret from her. That set off a chain of events that led to my current situation. My husband moved out because I admitted to loving another man. I'm forced to share my daughter with a woman I want to strangle like a Thanksgiving turkey. As I already mentioned, my sobriety is shot to hell now that I've made vodka the most important meal of the day.

My daughter, Bryann, is really struggling to deal with her feelings about Greg leaving our home. I guess I am too. Though he does not light my fire sexually and our emotional bond is not exactly covalent, he has been in my life for nearly two decades. That is supposed to count for something, right? He and I have yet to figure out if we are going to stay married or call it quits. If I am honest with myself, the only reason I would want him back is to put our family back together. I do not miss him. I miss our family.

To think that I destroyed my perfect little family unit for the likes of Kane Taylor makes me sick to my stomach every time I think of it. I allowed myself to feel emotion and fall in love with a man that I knew was a player of sorts. And what do I know about players? Players lie. They have to be good liars by definition. So what started off as a fun game of "cat and mouse" landed me in his trap with a broken home and a broken heart. But, I will never admit to the latter.

I do not know if Greg and I will get back together and I certainly have my hands full with trying to get back sober while guiding my daughter through this mess of a family. I've been trying to talk this out with myself and I'm getting nowhere so I have committed to find a loyal, trusted colleague to help me figure this whole thing out objectively.

For now, I'm on my way to my daughter's birthday luncheon. Bryann is turning fifteen today. Greg and I went all the way to South Africa to get our baby girl so we could give her a real family experience, like the ones on TV.   Little did we know, Bryann's birthmother also went all the way to South Africa to give her baby away in secret. Life is funny that way. Now, Bryann has a family not unlike one on the soap operas. I should have been more specific in my wishes about what kind of TV family I wanted.

So I am graciously hosting a small gathering today for Bryann's birthday. My two best friends who are her only "aunties" and Riley Briggs — the woman who brought my house down — are all having lunch together. Somehow I have got to figure out how to fit this woman in my daughter's life in a healthy way. As a trained, award-winning psychiatrist, I know I can build something healthy out of this mess.

They say keep your friends close and your enemies closer. I plan to keep Riley Briggs even closer than my enemies. She can interact with my daughter but I watch her very closely. We have already seen the destruction Riley can cause in the lives of people when she sets her mind to it. Somehow I have to grow a family tree out of all these broken twigs and branches for Bryann's sake. Maybe it is for my sake, too. Maybe when I look at Riley I see a little bit of myself the way Greg's mother saw herself in me when I was younger. For that reason, I will keep a close eye on Riley Briggs.

As a psychiatrist I have seen a lot of messy situations in my career. But I have to say, this very well might be the filthiest mess I have ever seen or heard of in my nearly twenty years of studying family chaos. They say a "rolling stone gathers no moss" meaning that people (usually men) can simply keep it moving through life without any attachments. All the broken pieces of bastard children, half-siblings, distant cousins, and unknown aunties just roll right under the feet of a rolling stone. But I am no rolling stone. I plan to gather up all this moss and make a family tree for my daughter. I make it sound so easy, don't I?

-1-

Farah was unsure how she would ever make it through the afternoon luncheon. She felt her stomach drop when she arrived at the restaurant and saw her daughter's birthmother standing out front. Riley always managed to pull off a look that was both trashy, yet amazingly graceful all at once. In a dress that appeared to be airbrushed onto her perfectly fit body, she showcased a plunging neckline and a hemline that cupped her buttocks.

"Hey Ladies!" Riley shouted.

"Hi Riley," Farah said while inhaling a deep cleansing breath.

Of course, Liv extended a welcoming hug to Riley. She was always the peacemaker and Farah knew that if she was going to be able to pull off this luncheon she would have to lean on Liv's grace.

Callie, on the other hand, simply nodded in Riley's direction. She had yet to get over all of Riley's antics from a few months ago. Callie had conducted a full investigation into Riley's sordid past. There was nothing criminal but certainly a long list of sketchy, questionable social behavior. Riley's behavior with men made escorts and call girls wince.

"Happy Birthday! How's my girl?" Riley asked Bryann. "Oh I see you are wearing the dress I bought you. Do you like it?"

Bryann looked at Farah. "Ummm, yeah. It's not something I would usually wear but I'm open to it."

"Good!" Riley said and smoothed her hands down her hips and thighs. "You have the same amazing body I have so we have to teach you how to flaunt it."

"Oh I am not so sure that is necessary at fifteen," Farah interjected.

"Please! Fifteen in some cultures is considered a women who can marry and bear children." Riley said with a smile to Bryann.

Farah saw Bryann's discomfort building. She did not want her daughter to be tense or upset for her birthday, or any other day for that matter. So Farah took another deep breath and smiled, "I suppose you are right, but my fifteen year old daughter will not be one of them."

"OUR daughter," Riley corrected her.

With that comment, Callie abruptly called out to the good-looking older gentleman standing behind the podium. "Excuse me handsome. We are the Goodwyn party of five."

The gentleman blushed and instructed the girls to follow him to a private room just off of the patio. It was a beautiful cozy room that could probably accommodate ten people, but for the day it was just the five of them. When Bryann entered the room she gasped.

"Mom! I love it." She leaned into Farah and gave her a tight hug. Farah felt the love of Bryann penetrate her bones. Bryann was the first thing in Farah's life that ever mattered to her. So making her happy each and every day was a priority. "Oh my goodness! Purple and pink butterflies everywhere. Thank you Mommy!"

"You're very welcome baby! Let's all sit down."

The waiter moved in and out of the room quickly. He returned with five champagne flutes. Bryann's eyes lit up like a diamonds before the waiter said, "Birthday girl…your sparkling cider." He bowed as if she were a princess.

"Mom!"

"Yes?" Farah looked at her.

"Oh come on Farah. It's her birthday. If she lived in Europe she could drink a year ago." Riley grabbed a glass from the waiter and placed it in front of Bryann who grinned.

Farah cleared her throat and the waiter retrieved the glass from in front of Bryann and placed it in front of Liv who quickly swallowed it before grabbing another. "Okay, here we go," Liv said under her breath.

Callie remained quiet but her eyes shot flaming arrows across the table at Riley. Farah began to wonder if this luncheon was a good idea. If these ladies could not make it though a two-hour lunch together there was no way they could spend the next twelve months planning Bryann's sweet sixteen.

After everyone had full glasses Farah proposed a toast. "Happy Birthday to my beautiful baby girl…" she looked over at Riley. "The sweet daughter that we all share. Baby, we are all here together as the women who love you. You can come to us for anything."

"…Anything," Callie interrupted assertively and shot a side eye at Riley.

Farah continued, "You have become such a wonderful young woman. You are an excellent student and wonderful friend to others…"

"…When I'm taking my meds," Bryann interrupted.

Farah felt her frustration building. She could not get through an affirming toast without someone interjecting a negative tone. "As I was saying… I'm very proud to be your mother. The day we brought you home was the best day of my life. And your dad's life too."

"Yes, how is ol' Greg," Riley sneered.

"Okay, that's it!" Callie snarled.

Riley snapped at Callie, "Oh I know you don't like me detective. You think I don't see you sitting there with those skinny little lips pursed together so tight you can't swallow? I see you. I just don't care how you feel about me."

"Good, because I can't stand the sight of you." Callie folded her arms and looked at Farah to continue.

"Just forget the toast…" Farah said, "Drink up everyone!"

It seemed like Farah and Liv raced to see who could finish the glass of champagne the fastest before grabbing the bottle from the ice bucket to pour more. When the waiter saw them pouring he walked over from the corner of the room. "Ladies, I'm here to do that for you."

"Well, you need to stand a little closer to the table then to get here fast enough," Liv laughed.

Bryann frowned at Farah as the waiter filled her mother's glass again. "Mom, are you having a third glass?"

"This is my second."

"I know," Bryann said. "I'm asking if you will be having a third."

"Ohhhh is that your way of telling me that this needs to be my last one?" Farah said in question.

"Yeah," Bryann said. "If I can't drink. You can't drink."

Farah laughed. "Thank you for your concern but you cannot drink by law. I cannot drink by genetic disorder. I have a choice. You, my darling, do not." Farah leaned over and kissed Bryann on the cheek.

"Your mom is right," Callie said.

"Here we go," Liv added.

"Yes, Liv, here we go. If I recall you were the one that started this whole thing anyway." Callie waited for Liv's response.

"I beg your pardon?" Liv tossed back another glass of champagne.

"You heard me! If you had never given her those cosmos, Farah's nearly ten years of sobriety would still be in tact." Callie charged.

"Wow! Some friend you are," Riley said to Liv.

Liv and Callie responded in unison, "What!"

"If you had never hired your cousin to destroy my marriage I would have had no need to drink." Farah snapped at Riley.

"Oh give me a break Farah. Take ownership of your mistakes. Will you? I had Kane approach you. You started sleeping with him all on your own. You destroyed your marriage. Not me. All I did was want to see my daughter."

"…whom you decided to give away and then changed your mind fifteen years later I guess," Bryann said. She shouted, "Look! It's my birthday and I don't want to hear any of this stuff. I want a drink and I could use a joint right now. Aunt Liv you got anything?"

The four ladies all sat erect in shock. Farah stared at her daughter unable to speak before collecting her thoughts. "Bryann, we've been through this over and over again. You are well medicated. You know very well that your behavior right now is unacceptable." Farah barked. "This is tough for everyone involved and especially for the people at this table. You owe Riley an apology."

"What!" Bryann and Callie groaned in unison.

Farah cut her eyes at Callie. Then responded to Bryann, "Yes, you owe her an apology. You are only fifteen years old. You have no idea about the complexities of womanhood and the tough decisions you will face as an adult. We all do the very best we can and sometimes..." Farah looked over at Riley, "Sometimes, we screw it up."

"That's true," Liv hiccupped. She had taken a full bottle of champagne for herself and pulled a flask of vodka from her designer bag.

Bryann sighed, "Like you cheated on dad?"

Bryann began to cry and Farah felt her vision start to blur in anger at Riley. It was her presence that caused all of the confusion. Before Riley Briggs walked into their world everything was fine. At least it felt fine.

"Yes baby. I cheated on dad. It was my mistake but Riley and Kane tricked me. I've apologized to your dad and I'm apologizing to you."

"Kane didn't trick you," Riley said. "Kane loves you."

"Oh Dear Lord," Callie shouted and threw her hands in the air.

"I knew it!" The Liv said. She was a sucker for love. "I knew he really loved you. I could see it in his eyes at court.

He sounded so sincere on that witness stand. When a woman is in love it's in her smile. When a man is in love it's in his eyes."

"He was sincere," Riley said.

"I don't care." Farah folded her arms with a scowl.

"Do you think you and Dad will get back together," Bryann asked Farah.

"I don't know, honey."

"Why don't you know?" Bryann asked.

Riley answered for Farah, "Because she loves Kane, who is your cousin too, by the way."

Farah, Callie and Liv are grunted in sorts. "Damn! I never thought of that," Liv giggled.

"Why are you laughing?" Callie frowned.

Liv hiccupped. "I don't know," she paused, "because I'm drunk." She giggled again.

"What else is new," Bryann said under her breath.

Liv dipped her brows at her goddaughter with a harsh frown. "What did your mother just tell you? Little girl, you wait and see. Being a grown up woman is not as easy as you think. Dealing with men and kids and family and just mess! Mess! Mess!"

"She's right sweetie," Callie said to Bryann. "Don't ever judge another woman's actions and behavior because you probably don't know her story."

Callie dropped her head. Farah and Liv got quiet and the table became very still. Riley looked back and forth among the long faces at the table.

"What? What am I missing?" Riley asked.

"It's not really any of your business Miss Riley," Bryann said with tone. Her face dropped and the brazen teenager from a few moments ago returned to the sweet little girl they all knew. "Sorry Auntie Liv. I'm sorry Aunt Callie. Sorry Mom."

Farah smiled at Bryann. Callie lifted her eyes just long enough to flash a slight grin toward her goddaughter and Liv leaned in and blew Bryann a kiss from across the table.

"Ahem," Riley cleared her throat. "What about me?"

"I can't say I'm sorry to you Miss Riley…" Bryann said.

"And can't you call me something else?"

"Miss Riley." Bryann repeated. "I don't apologize to you. I cannot judge that you gave me away as a baby but I can judge the way you came back and tried to ruin my mom and dad. For that I don't forgive you."

Riley looked at Farah who remained stoic and trying not to twist her lips in agreement with her daughter. Farah was proud of Bryann's response. She could make Bryann respect Riley's decision to pursue adoption but she could not force her daughter to ignore the feelings she had about Riley being back in her life.

"I don't even know why you came back," Bryann said.

Everyone at the table waited for Riley's response. Riley leaned back in her chair and Farah could see her chest rise and fall. Riley was anxious and Farah could see that Riley was torn about whether or not she wanted to tell the truth. This was the benefit to Farah being a psychiatrist. Her psychoanalysis skills did not leave her when she walked out of the office.

Riley looked up at the sky. "Well, I'll admit that when I first came back around I just wanted to get your attention."

"Why?" Bryann asked her.

"Because I was trying to get your dad's….Kendall's attention."

"The guy from the courtroom? With the wife?" Callie asked.

Riley nodded. "We've been together for years and we love each other very much. He's my whole world. But he is married. At one point we were both married, but I ended my marriage. He was supposed to end his too."

"Of course," Liv said. "All married men claim they are leaving their wives."

"No! I believe he was. Then Lorraine, his wife, got pregnant."

"She GOT pregnant?" Callie asked. "He had a hand in that didn't he?"

Riley sat for a minute. She had never thought of it that way. Kendall had been sleeping with both Lorraine and

Riley at the same time. He was probably still sleeping with both of them. Riley felt herself getting upset. "Well, whatever! However it happened. She threatened him and made him stay."

"And you stayed with him," Farah asked her. At this point, Riley had the attention of everyone at that table. Farah believed that this was the moment Riley became a member of the family. She could tell that Callie and Liv were looking at Riley in a different way. They looked at her as if she were human, rather than the unfeeling, destructive monster Riley loved to portray.

"I left him initially, but I love him. I can't stay away from him." Riley paused and smiled at Bryann. "You were conceived in love, my dear. So from Kendall and I to your parents you have been the object of a lot of love."

Bryann leaned over and gave Riley a hug. There was not a dry eye at the table. The waiter in the corner even wiped beneath his eye. For the rest of the lunch they ate, drank and laughed at the perils of being women. Farah even allowed Bryann to have a mimosa that was heavy on OJ.

As the cake arrived the girls sang "Happy Birthday" to Bryann. Bryann squealed when she saw the pink and purple glitter cake in the shape of a butterfly. She looked around the table and prepared to make her wish. She stood up over the fifteen pink and purple butterfly candles.

"I wish that I can grow up to be as awesome as you guys and I wish my mom and dad get back together." Bryann blew out her candles.

Farah dropped her head. "We'll see baby."

"Do you love him," Riley asked Farah.

"I was married to him for nearly twenty years," Farah said with an annoyance in her voice.

"But do you love him?" Riley asked.

Farah looked over at Bryann and formed the lie in her mouth. "Absolutely," Farah responded with contrived confidence.

"Then you can make it work," Riley smiled. She cleared her throat. "I'm sorry Farah. I'm sorry for what I did to you and Greg."

Farah looked at her. She could not speak but she nodded in thanks.

As the girls were wrapping up a voice called in through the main doorway, "Olive? Olive Jones?"

Liv turned around towards the door and threw both hands over her mouth. She had not seen him in years but the moment she laid eyes on him it all the emotion came flooding back to her.

"Uh Oh," Callie said to Farah who did not recognize the man.

Liv got up from the table and Farah leaned over to Callie, "Who is that?"

"That's Dylan!"

"Oh Damn!"

"Yeah, oh damn is right."

"We have to do something," Farah said.

Callie and Farah turned toward the door and saw Liv and Dylan embracing in a way that seemed comfortable, familiar and destined to happen again. Before Callie and Farah could think Liv and Dylan approached the table.

"Ladies, you remember Dylan," Liv said smiling.

"Yes," Callie and Farah said with fake smiles.

"It is good to see you ladies again." Dylan smiled and the shine of his eyes eclipsed the sun. He was indeed one of the most beautiful people ever created by God. He was a perfect physical specimen and Liv was madly in love with him at one point in her life.

Farah responded, "Likewise."

Callie did not say a word. She only rolled her eyes.

Dylan smiled at Callie, "Detective Piper, it has been a long time, huh?"

"Yup!" Callie responded. "The last time I saw you I was pulling a knife from your wife's hand. How is ol' Hannah Lecter these days?"

"Callie!" Liv shouted. She turned to Dylan. "I'm sorry."

"No problem. I understand." Dylan extended his hand to Callie. "Well, you will be happy to know that I am no longer married to Hannah 'Lecter', as you call her. She is long gone and there is no one to ride on top of cars, jump out of bushes or pull knives on this beautiful woman right here."

The smile stretched across Liv's face was intense. It was as if she was falling back in love with every single word that slid from his mouth. Liv was obsessed with Dylan. He was the first and last man she had an affair with while married to Adam. He was the last because Liv was so broken-hearted afterwards that she swore she would never cheat again.

Liv was willing to leave her marriage for Dylan. She was in love. However, Dylan would not leave his mentally ill wife. He loved Liv but he was committed to his wife, Hannah. That was eight years ago.

Suddenly Riley stood to her feet and smoothed her dress as if there was any room for it to wrinkle. "Riley Briggs and you are?" She said in a sultry seductive tone just above a whisper.

"Dylan Jaxson," he said. "The great love of Olive's life."

Riley put a devious and sarcastic grin on her face. "Hmm, I thought Adam was the love of her life. Silly me." Riley leaned in to the table to show Dylan her cleavage. "Well, I'm just learning all kinds of new things today."

Dylan cleared his throat and moved his attention away from Riley. "So it is your birthday today. You must be Bryann."

"I am," she said. "And you must be crazy."

"Bryann!" Liv said. "What did we just talk about today?"

"Okay. Okay." Bryan extended her hand. "Hello Mr. Jaxson."

"Boy this is a tough crowd. It is feeling all Oprah woman power up in here."

"Yes it is," Callie laughed.

Riley pulled a card from her clutch handbag. "Dylan darling, please give me a call. I could do some things with you."

Liv bit her lip. "Excuse me?"

Riley raised her eyebrows. "Yes, Mrs. Jones? Is there a problem?"

Liv looked over at Bryann. "No. No problem at all. You guys are both single and it doesn't look like Kendall is ever going to leave his wife so knock yourself out."

"Damn!" Riley laughed and nodded in approval of Liv's jab at her. "That was pretty good. You like him that much, huh Liv?" Riley winked at Dylan. "Call me." She licked her lips and sat back down.

He ignored Riley's advance, which was quite shocking to her ego. "Well ladies, it was great to see you again. Happy

Birthday young lady and… um… nice to meet you Riley." Dylan kissed Liv on the cheek, placed Riley's card on the table in front of her and walked away.

They all watched Dylan walk with swag that seemed to move the door toward him rather than him moving toward the doorway. When he was inside the doorway he turned around to see everyone watching him. He chuckled. "Call me Olive. I really miss you."

-2-

Farah opened the door and was surprised to see Greg standing there. Physically he was still the most attractive man she had ever laid eyes upon in her life. From the day she spotted him on campus to that very moment, Greg was a creation of physical perfection from head to toe. He was gorgeous, sexy, and powerful. Yet, she had no butterflies in her stomach for him. She had no tingle between her thighs. But she did have a flutter in her heart.

"Oh, hey," Farah said. She looked at Greg with a question spread across her face.

"Why do you look so shocked? I told you I would be here at seven," he said.

Farah stuttered. "I..I know but I did not expect you to ring the bell. Why didn't you use your key?"

"Because I don't live here."

"You pay the mortgage."

"I do," Greg nodded. He stood on the outside of the home he designed especially for his wife years ago. He believed it was their dream home. Now it had become a treasure chest of their memories, but not their home. "But, I do not live here."

Farah swung the door open the rest of the way and signaled for her estranged husband to step inside. She could see the pain on his face as he walked through the foyer into the family room. He looked around the room as if he expected her to have changed everything the moment he walked out the door.

"Well, things are still the same," Greg said with a polite smile.

"Not exactly," Farah said. She offered him a slight grin.

"How so?" he asked.

Farah looked at him with doe eyes, "You are missing."

Greg frowned. "Farah, please don't do this."

She smiled, now showing just a few teeth. "No, No. I won't. I promise." Her eyes started to gloss over and she felt a lump in her throat.

"Why are you going to cry?" Greg asked.

"I'm not," she said.

"Farah, I know you. You are holding back tears." Greg looked at Farah like his arms were wrapped around her shoulders. He wanted to place her head on his chest and tell her it would be okay. But he was unsure of whether it actually would be. "Talk to me. Why are you sad?"

"Why am I sad?" Farah mocked. "Greg, you moved out of our home. You've leased an apartment, got a new car, and probably a new girlfriend." Farah dropped her eyes.

"Don't be ridiculous!" he said.

Farah looked up at him. "Is that so ridiculous, Greg? You are so hot I know that women are falling at your feet."

He chuckled, "Yes, I've garnered some attention. But there is only one woman I've ever wanted in my life. That is you."

"Then why did you leave?" A tear finally fell down Farah's cheek.

Greg felt his stomach fall. He wanted to hold Farah tight, but he was determined to change her behavior. He gathered his emotion. "I have suffered enough of your selfish behavior. I am tired of all the affairs and irresponsible sexual escapades. Baby, I understand you had a tough past with your Aunt Janice. I do. But, it's been long enough for you to heal. For God's sake, Farah, you are a psychiatrist! You do this for a living. You can fix everyone else but yourself!" Greg's voice and tone escalated and made Farah cry harder.

Greg's words penetrated Farah and she pulled her shoulders back. Farah cleared her throat and dried her eyes. "You're right. Let's just talk about Bryann's Sweet Sixteen."

"Her birthday was just a few days ago. Do we really need to talk about this now?"

Farah not only wanted to talk about it now. She needed to talk about it to shift the conversation away from the marriage and her failure. She sniffed and wiped her nose on the shoulder of her t-shirt. "Greg, this is like planning a wedding for our daughter. It's the rehearsal for the big thing when she eventually finds the love of her life." Farah swallowed hard. "It's going to take us a year to do this right."

"Okay, a year of time and how much money?" Greg saw the smile in Farah's puffy eyes and knew he was going to be in for a bunch of money. It always cost him five figures whenever Farah or Bryann gave him the dazzling eyes. This time was no different.

"Ten grand," Farah said smiling in her eyes. The tracks of her tears still lingered and her nose was still tinted red through her brown skin but the joy of planning her daughter's Sweet Sixteen party shone through all of that.

"Ten thousand dollars!" Greg shouted.

"Yes! This is a big deal. It's like a wedding."

"But it's NOT a wedding, Farah. Don't you think that's a bit excessive?"

"No," Farah looked at Greg with resolve in her eyes. "This is our only daughter. She only turns sixteen once and after all that she has been through over these past few months she deserves a huge, spectacular, off the chart celebration."

"She does or you do?" he asked.

"Both of us do."

Greg laughed in a way that he had not in many months. "I see. So where is the teen princess, anyway?" He spoke the words inside of a continued chuckle.

"She's with Riley."

Greg's laughter came to an immediate halt. "What did you say?"

"You heard me. She's with Riley."

"Why is she with that woman?"

Farah exhaled and counted to three in her head. "Bryann wants to get to know her birthmother. She wants to know how they are similar. She wants to understand what she was born with, what Riley gave her."

"Bipolar disorder. Mystery solved."

"Greg!" Farah frowned, "Yes, it seems that Bryann's problems and Riley's life are certainly linked to one another. But we already knew that our daughter's mental illness was genetic. She wants to know about other things like the way she twitches her lips when she's embarrassed or the way her nose turns red when she tells a lie."

"Well, we know Riley's nose does not turn red when she lies. Otherwise, she would walk around looking like Bozo the clown…"

Farah laughed, "…or Rudolph the red-nosed reindeer."

Greg joined Farah in a hearty burst of laughter that ended with them locking eyes with a smile. Farah quickly brushed the moment off of her like a flake of dandruff. She did not want to get back into the emotional boxing ring with Greg.

"So, we can have the ten thousand?"

Greg thought for a moment. "Farah, you are a brilliant psychiatrist with a successful practice. You have ten thousand dollars. You have ten thousand dollars many times over. Why are you asking me about this?"

"You know I put all my money right back into the practice."

"Wait! You still don't pay yourself a salary?" Greg looked shocked.

"No. I've never paid myself a salary." Farah said.

Greg shook his head. "As hard as you work, how can you work for free."

Farah smiled, "Because I have a husband who provides a life for me that I can do what I enjoy and get good people on my staff to work around me. I've got the best psychologists, coaches and social workers in the business because I can offer them full health insurance, paid vacation and sick days."

Greg nodded. "Yeah, you do."

"And it's only because of you, honey. Without your love and support all these years I could have never built up the practice to what it is today."

Greg felt his heart warm. Farah felt her chest rise. Neither of them said anything for nearly a minute that seemed like hours. Finally Greg said, "And you repaid me by falling in love with a package delivery guy."

Just that quickly the moment was gone again. Farah knew Greg was right. She had been so unfair to him for all of these years. She looked for fulfillment outside of her marriage. Sure, she had her reasons but none of them justified hurting Greg the way she had over the years. He worshipped her. She had grown to love him so much that her love transferred from romantic to familial, brotherly love. Then, the sex ended and life began.

"Greg, I'm sorry."

"You still see him?" Greg asked with a scowl.

"No! Absolutely not."

"Hmm, interesting."

"What's interesting?"

"Well, a few months ago you sat in that same spot on the sofa and told me you loved him. Now you do not speak to him. Weird."

"It's not weird. I fell in love with a person that does not exist. He tricked me. He made it all up to woo me away from you."

"And it worked." Greg said. He stood up from his chair. "Just let me know what you need for Bryann's party.

But please do not ask me about colors, napkins, flowers, or any of that stuff. I'm strictly here to write checks."

"What else is new?" Farah said under her breath.

"Huh?" Greg turned towards her as they walked back to the front of the house.

"I just said what else is new that you are only writing checks."

"What do you mean by that?" he asked.

Farah looked at him in his eyes. "All you care about is making money. Writing checks for things."

"I do that because I love my girls."

"Yes, but sometimes we wanted you Greg. We did not always want the check with us. Sometimes we wanted you."

The way Farah said the word "you" made Greg think. Up until that moment he felt he had done nothing to warrant Farah's behavior throughout their marriage. He considered her affairs just immature ways to reclaim the youth that was stolen by her mother and father's absence. Just then, Greg realized that he had neglected his wife. After he married her, he focused on caring for her and giving her anything she wanted.

"Wow," Greg said just above a whisper. "I'm sorry, Cutie."

Farah looked up at him. "You are?"

"I am," Greg finally allowed himself to put his arms around Farah. He held her in close. "I never knew you felt that way."

"But I've told you many times." Farah spoke into the comfort of Greg's chest.

"Well, I guess this is the first time I heard you," he said.

Greg lifted Farah's chin and it reminded her of Kane's touch. But when she looked into Greg's eyes she saw a future and a past. She felt a connection that she had not felt with him in many years. Greg and Bryann were her life and she wanted her life back.

"Listen, Mom and Dad are hosting their anniversary party. Well, actually Acer and I are hosting," he said in air quotes, "but mom is doing all the planning. She just put our names on the invite. Will you come with me?" Greg looked at Farah with expectation. He was not presumptuous.

"Oh, I don't know…"

"Farah, please. My parents do not know we are separated."

"They don't?"

"Of course not. You think I want to hear my mother's mouth about how I should have never married a black girl."

Farah pulled her head back and pointed at Greg. "Aha! So you admit your mother is racist." She waited for his reply.

"Baby, we both know my mother is racist. I don't know why it has always been so important for you to hear me say it."

"Hmmm, okay, I'll go. But, you have to get Callie and Liv an invite as well."

"Of course, Adam is my best friend. He and Olive are already on the list."

"And Callie…?"

Greg sighed, "Can I check with Acer first. I don't want any trouble between the two of them."

"Oh please! She's over him. She has been over your little brother since the day they broke up." She laughed.

"There are two sides to every story, Dr. Goodwyn." Greg chuckled.

"True, but we know your brother."

"And we know Callie."

"Touche'" Farah nodded and they laughed. "It could go either way."

"But I'll talk to him and see how he feels."

Farah had a thought and she wanted to run it by Greg as he walked through the doorway. "Hey!"

He turned around. "What do you think about inviting Riley?"

"WHAT! Have you gone mad?"

"She's apart of our family now. That would be a great place for her to meet everybody all together."

"And who shall we say she is, pray tell." Greg said sternly in a tone and inflection that reminded Farah of her father-in-law.

"Well, Judge Goodwyn…" Farah mocked Greg's voice and tried to imitate his father, "I'd say we ought tell them the bloody truth. She is Bryann's birth mummy."

"Very funny," Greg said. He stood for a moment and thought about what Farah said earlier. This was an opportunity for him to be present and supportive emotionally. "I don't agree but I will go along with it for the sake of Bryann."

Farah leaped into his arms. "Thank you, Greg!" She kissed him on the lips and after an awkward moment he placed her back to the floor.

"Don't say I didn't warn you though. That woman is trouble." Greg kissed Farah on the cheek and made his way down the walkway.

Farah stood in the doorway and watched as her husband pulled off in his new shiny black sports car. She wondered what his new apartment looked like on the inside. Greg was never one to pay attention to decorating or details outside of numbers so she could only imagine him sitting in an empty white-walled room with a sofa, a television and an elliptical. She made a mental note to ask Bryann about her father's apartment.

She waved goodbye to Greg. Just as she closed the front door her phone vibrated. She prayed it was not the hospital calling with an emergency. When she picked up her phone she saw, "DO NOT ANSWER". She knew exactly who it was. She threw the phone onto the sofa and went into the kitchen to make herself a drink.

She walked back into the family room with her chilled cosmo, Kane had called her twenty-three times already that day. The phone rang one last time and she answered with rage in her voice. "What!"

"Farah? Hello."

"What do you want? Why are you ringing my phone off the hook?"

"I just want to talk to you," Kane said. His voice was deep, slow, and solemn.

"I have nothing to say to you," she paused. "EVER AGAIN!"

"Farah, please! I love you. Don't do this to me. To us."

"There is no us, you pathological liar."

"Farah, please."

"Don't 'Farah please' me! Do not call me ever again."

"I want to make love to you. I know you are hurt." Kane's words struck lightning between Farah's thighs, but she ignored him.

Farah paused. "Kane, get the hell off of my phone. When I think of us making love it makes me vomit."

"Damn babe. It's like that."

"YES! It is exactly LIKE THAT!" Farah slammed the phone down on the table as if she had hung up a land line. She stomped across the room and heard Kane's voice.

"Hello. Hello."

"Ugh!" Farah shouted. She scurried across the room, picked up the phone and ended the call. Then she stomped up the stairs to her room. She thought about the nerve of him. "What an idiot!" She said aloud.

Farah thought about what Riley said at the luncheon. She said that Kane really loved Farah. That did not matter to Farah. She had just had an amazing couple of hours with Greg and knew that she wanted her family back. She was not interested in some lying, scheming package delivery guy.

Farah flopped on the bed and Kane's voice rang through her mind. "I want to make love to you." She tossed from one side to the other. He thighs rubbed together. She crossed her arms tight. She was so turned on by his persistence and his composure even when she was screaming at him like a wild woman. He knew just how to calm her down. So many times during their courtship he made love to her and changed her whole outlook on the day. Kane's touch was fire. His voice was soothing. His thrust was like the ocean as it gently, but forcefully crashing onto the shore.

Farah exhaled slowly. She closed her eyes and thought of the last time she and Kane made love. It was on her kitchen floor. Sure, it was a bold move but Greg had moved out and she was hurting. Farah relaxed her shoulders and sank her head into her pillow. She unconsciously licked her lips and thought of sucking on Kane.

Before she knew it, Farah had reached into the nightstand and dusted off those toys that Greg once loved. He complained that they had an arsenal of erotica in their bedroom and never used any of it. Well, Farah decided that day it was time to get back to business. She pulled out the most intense vibrator she had and pulled her sweat pants completely off. She lay in her panties and rubbed her stomach thinking of Kane. Then, she turned on her vibrator and pleasured herself to sleep.

-3-

When the officer knocked at Riley's window she rolled her eyes and pushed the button to lower the window. To her delight, the officer was an exceptionally handsome Hispanic man. "Probably Dominican," she thought.

His biceps bulged through his uniform shirt and his chest looked like he had been bench-pressing tree trunks. His hair was freshly cut and he smelled like he just stepped out of the shower lathered in Irish Spring.

"Well, hello officer," Riley said. She made sure to stick her cleavage where he could see it.

"Ma'am you can't sit here. You have to park in the garage or drive around until your party arrives."

"Looks like to me the party has arrived," she paused to look at his name badge, "Officer Santiago". The officer smiled. His teeth were perfectly straight with just a slight gap in the front. *Got him!* Riley thought to herself.

The officer chuckled, "I knew when I saw you that you were a party girl."

Riley dipped her head as if she was embarrassed. "You did?"

"Yup!" The officer grinned with pride.

"Well, how did you know that? What gave me away?" Riley bit her bottom lip and pouted just long enough for his eyes to fall down into her blouse.

"This car for starters. It's so sexy."

Riley smiled big. She had finally persuaded Kendall to get her a BMW 6 series. It was the third car he had gifted to her during their relationship. Riley told Kendall she always needed two cars, a black one and a white one, so she could match her car with her moods. Sometimes she was a "good girl" and drove the white Mercedes CLK Kendall bought her for her 30th birthday. Most times, the quintessential bad girl, she drove the black CLK he bought her as a peace offering after their first big fight. She was tired of driving two of the same car. So she kept the white CLK and Kendall bought her a black BMW.

"Thanks," Riley said, "I love my new car."

"Oh you just got it. No wonder you are showcasing. Well, maybe you can take me for a ride one day."

Riley winked at him, "You got it." She saw Kendall coming up in the rear view mirror.

Officer Santiago leaned into the car window. Meanwhile, many other cars also took advantage of Riley's calculated conversation skills by pulling up curbside and waiting for loved ones. "So can I get your number?"

Riley saw Kendall approaching. "Sure let me give you my card." She pulled a red and black business card from inside her bra. "Here you go. Call me."

He nodded, "Will do. Hey, sorry I can't let you just sit here."

"Oh no problem," Riley said as Kendall opened the passenger side door.

Kendall looked at the officer and smiled. "Tell me you didn't let her stall you until I got out here." He laughed in a deep bellow.

Riley winked at the officer and leaned over to kiss Kendall. The officer stood up straight. "I guess I did," he said in a tone that mixed authoritative power with disappointment.

Riley put the car in drive and mouthed to the officer quietly, "Call me." She and Kendall drove off.

"Did you just tell him to call you?" Kendall asked.

"Are you married?" Riley responded.

Kendall frowned. He let out a long sigh. "How are you baby girl? How was your week?"

"It was actually really good. I think I found a broker that I like and I've started the process of getting my license for the tri-state."

"Tri-State?"

"Yeah. New York, New Jersey, and Connecticut."

"That's great, sweetie. I'm proud of you. It sounds like you are getting settled in your new life as a New Yorker."

"Yeah, but I really miss Stormy. At some point I hope to move my mother up here, too."

Kendall squinted. "You do?"

Riley laughed. "Not really, but it sounded like the right thing to say."

Kendall looked at her and Riley felt her cheeks turn flush. After all these years, he still had the same effect on her as the very first time they met. Kendall started out as Riley's mentor in the real estate game but before he knew it, she had trapped him in her web. They had been deep, soulful lovers ever since.

"So I have something to tell you," Kendall said.

"Uh Oh," Riley frowned, "Can it wait until we get to the apartment?"

"Well, I wanted to wait but by the looks of this traffic that could be hours from now."

"I told you not to arrive during rush hour," Riley said in irritation. "Getting back through the tunnel to Manhattan at this time of day is brutal."

"Calm down. It's okay. I enjoy sitting here next to you. I like watching you showcase your East Coast driving skills."

She laughed, "Yeah, I'm learning." Riley took the opportunity to quickly cut over in front of the car in the next lane. She threw up her hand as if the driver actually invited her in front. "Thanks!"

"So do you want to hear my big news or not?"

"If it's not that you are leaving Lorraine then anything else is not really big news. So, probably not." She smiled at him and blew a kiss.

Kendall shook his head and smiled. "Not quite that big but I think you'll like it."

"Okay try me."

"I told Lorraine we are not moving to California…."

Riley's smile spread across her face and across the tri-state. "YOU DID!!!"

"I did," he said. "See, I told you that you would like it."

"I do. I do." Riley zipped through traffic and wedged in front of another car going back to her original lane. "If I wasn't in all this traffic I would stop and kiss you right now!"

Kendall leaned over to her. "So how about I just kiss you." He brushed his lips across her cheek. "I love you, baby girl."

"I love you too, papa bear."

***

It took nearly an hour and a half but Riley and Kendall finally got back to her apartment. She never really adjusted to the tiny living space and the large monthly payment. In the Midwest, an apartment of the same size would be less than half of what it is in New York. But, with all the access to everything she needed it was worth every penny to her. Especially, since Kendall paid the rent.

Kendall dropped his bag at the door and Riley picked it up and handed it to him. "In the bedroom please," she paused, "you act like you have to walk more than ten steps to get there."

"Yes dear." He walked to the bedroom that was actually only eight steps away from the front door. "I hope the places my guy shows us this weekend are much bigger than this," Kendall said. "This is ridiculous. I'm surprised you've been able to stay here this long."

"I'm so excited! I will have my own New York apartment. I feel like Carrie Bradshaw." Riley squealed. "And you're my Mr. Big."

She skipped across the room, leaped in his arms and gave him an open mouth kiss that caused a bulge in his pants. The love between Riley and Kendall was so natural, so passionate. So real.

It was also so wrong. Everybody knew it but the two of them. They conceived Bryann over fifteen years ago. They had been together probably about four to six months before that. The affair between them had lasted longer than most marriages.

It had outlasted Riley's marriage. She met Kendall when she was engaged to her ex-husband. She gave birth to Bryann while she planned her wedding. There was not a day of Riley's marriage that Kendall was not in her heart and on her mind. She finally decided to divorce Damon because she did not love him. This fact was not lost on Damon. He was well aware of all of Riley's escapades with numerous men, especially her longtime affair with Kendall. Her husband was willing to stay with her because he loved her, not because she loved him. But, Riley cared for him too much to watch him hurt.

She accepted her fate as a cursed woman. Her great-grandmother had told her that the men she loved would never love her. And the men who loved her, she would never love. Her entire family had been cursed for three generations. There were eight women with twenty-four husbands among them. Then her cousin married again and made it twenty-five. Riley's decision to divorce her ex-husband was par for the curse.

There was a knock at the door and Kendall immediately gave Riley the side eye. "Now who might that be?" he asked her with accusation in his voice.

"Oh please! It's probably Zo." Riley swung the door open. "Ta-da! See, just my dear cousin."

Kendall smiled, "Oh, Hey Zo!"

"Will you guys please stop calling me that? My name is Kane. I am a grown man. Nobody has called me Zo since I was in middle school."

"We still do," Riley snipped.

"I know and I've asked you to stop."

"Okay fine." Riley slammed the door.

Kane walked over to the sofa. He and Kendall locked hands and arms, pulled each other in to an embrace. "What's up my dude?" Kane said.

"Not a damn thing," Kendall responded.

"Can't you two just shake hands like regular people? What's with all the pulling and snapping and stuff?"

Kane laughed. "That would be the brotherhood handshake. You don't know about that. It's a handshake and a hug all in one."

"Well, I have never seen two white men do all that to shake hands." Riley said.

Kane replied, "Just because you haven't seen it does not mean it doesn't happen. You've also never seen them smoke weed or beat their wives but they do that, too. "

"You're terrible," Kendall laughed. "Your entire family goes to the next level to prove the their point. You guys crack me up with that."

"Well, you must love it because you've been here with us for a bunch of years now." Kane chuckled and flopped down in the chair next to the sofa.

"True that! This woman has me wrapped around her finger." Kendall lifted his chin to signal Riley for a kiss.

She bent down and kissed him and said, "…my naked finger."

"Here we go…" Kane laughed. "I don't understand women. How is it that you are still complaining that this guy is married? He's been married since the day you met him. Nothing has changed. Women complain about things they know existed in the beginning. As if magically it will disappear during the relationship."

Kendall responded, "Because they believe they can change us, man. Women are creatures of hope. For real, that's why you need a woman on your side. A woman's hope never diminishes. Then they use that hope to will your ass into whatever they hope for."

"That's deep," Kane nodded in agreement. "Yo! For real. That's good stuff right there."

Riley burst into laughter, "Okay Oprah and Iylana, if you guys are finished with relationship hour can we decide what we are going to order for dinner?"

"I'll leave it to you guys," Kendall said. "I'm going to go jump in the shower while you decide. I'm good with whatever. You know what I like baby." He kissed her before leaving the room.

Once Riley heard the water in the shower she whispered to Kane, "Listen, do not tell him about Bryann's sweet sixteen party."

"What? Why not?"

"No! I don't want him coming here with Lorraine and ruining my time with my daughter."

"It is his daughter, too." Kane reminded her.

"Yep, but not Lorraine's and I don't want her using some sister bonding shenanigans to bring that other little girl around Bryann right now."

"But, that is her sister, right?"

"Not really."

"What do you mean not really?" Kane shook his head. "You still haven't learned your lesson have you?"

"What lesson?" Riley asked.

"Exactly." Kane leaned in towards her with a whisper. "Riley, relationships are built on honesty and trust. When will you learn that your dishonesty is going to get you in trouble every time? If you don't tell Kendall about this party he is going to be angry with you."

"…And he's been angry with me before. You better not say a word. I mean it."

Kane continued to try to convince his cousin that she needed to be honest with Kendall about her feelings. He reminded her of all the ways her deception has backfired in the past.   Then, Riley heard the shower water stop. "I'm fine just the way I am. Thank you very much. Keep your mouth shut," she whispered.

Kendall's voice barged through the bathroom door and into the living room. "What did you guys decide?"

"Italian," Riley shouted back.

"Great choice," Kendall said before opening the door with a towel wrapped around his waist. "What did you order for me?"

"We haven't ordered yet."

"Seriously? I'm starving." He lifted his shoulders as if asking why she had not ordered the food.

"I know. Zo…uh I mean, Kane could not choose between Italian and American comfort food." Riley looked at Kane.

He returned her glance with a glare. "Yeah, sorry my dude," Kane said in a dry voice that made Riley grimace.

She mouthed to him in silence, "Sorry." Then shrugged her shoulders.

Kendall came back out into the living room wearing a pair of gym shorts and a white ribbed tank. He still had droplets of water on his shoulders. Riley inhaled his scent. He smelled clean with a citrus aroma but it was not overpowering. Kendall started putting lotion on his legs and arms. Then he looked at Kane.

"So, Kane, what's up with Farah? How is she?"

"She won't talk to me man."

"Well, give her time. That's to be expected. I'm sure all of this is a lot for her to handle. Her entire life just shifted. Is her husband still out of the house?"

"Yeah, I think so. But she will not talk to me so I don't really know what is going on. I called her the other day and she was so damn evil. Like a different person."

"She's hurt. Give her time. If she picked up the phone for you, then there is still hope for the two of you. Don't give up on her. Do not ever give up on the woman you love." Kendall advised.

Riley rolled her eyes. "You two sound like women. Blah. Blah. Blah."

"Ok, tough girl, we have made you uncomfortable talking about love." Kendall chuckled.

Kane laughed, "Yeah, you know Riley thinks love is for weaklings."

"Oh she does, does she?" Kendall laughed.

"No!" Riley injected. "I said love makes YOU a weakling, dear cousin. I asked you to do one simple thing. Instead, you go off and fall in love with the woman. Geesh!"

"Farah is a wonderful person," Kane said. "You should be glad since she is raising your daughter."

Riley sighed, "I am." She lowered her eyes. "You know, she invited me to lunch with them a couple of times now. I really had a good time with them for Bryann's birthday. I am not so sure how I feel about that Callista though."

"Yeah, Callie is not feeling me at all," Kane said.

"I know," Riley agreed. "She's not big on me either. I mean I like her style. She is direct and tells it like it is. But it is kind of weird to be with a white woman who looks white, acts white but knows so much about black culture."

Kendall raised his eyebrows, "Because her best friends are black."

"So are her parents," Kane added.

"Really?" Kendall said. "Wow."

Riley explained Callie's situation of being adopted by a Black family. "She is a lot different than some of the other chicks out there that try to emulate black culture. She's just a regular ol' white girl who happens to have a Black family and Black friends."

"Does she date brothers?" Kendall asked.

Kane answered, "She dates anybody from what I understand. She doesn't discriminate. She loves all men." Kane winked at Kendall. "That's probably why my cousin over there is not feeling her. They are too much alike."

"Cute." Riley smirked. "Well, I think Farah and I are more alike than Callie and me."

"Crazy! Farah is nothing like you," Kane roared in laughter.

"Ha! So you think." Riley smiled. "Farah is undercover with her stuff. We've seen that about her."

"Anyway, I'm just glad everyone is getting along in this madness. This situation is bananas." Kendall said.

"Yeah, we are all connected by a single thread that runs through all of us," Riley said.

"God?" Kane asked.

"No, ME!" Riley scoffed. "I gave birth to Bryann. I decided to come back for her. I hooked you to Farah."

Kane and Kendall looked at each other. At first neither one of them said anything but finally Kendall spoke up. "Baby girl, you did set off a chain of events here. No doubt. But only God could have come up with all of the connections in this mess."

"I'm not a church girl by any means. But I know enough not to include God in this mess. God had no part in us cheating, me getting pregnant, Farah cheating with Kane and him falling in love with a married woman. That's a whole lot of adultery for God to be involved."

"God is involved in everything, Riley."

"Wait a minute!" Riley raised her eyes at Kendall. "What is all this God talk? Since when do you think or talk about God. I tried to get you to go to church with me a hundred times. You never agreed to go with me."

Kane rolled his eyes. "Probably because of the reason you just outlined, silly. How is he going to be up in church with his mistress?"

Kendall sat on the sofa real solemn. He was deep in thought while Kane and Riley went back and forth on the merits of what to include and exclude from God. Finally he spoke and cut Kane off mid sentence.

"You are wrong man. Riley is not my mistress. I mean, she hasn't been my mistress in a long time."

Kane had a puzzled look on his face. "I don't follow."

"I love your cousin with all my heart…"

"Awww," Riley interrupted.

"…Let me finish baby girl." Kendall hushed her and Riley fell back in her seat. She knew he was serious. Kendall continued, "There was a brief time in the beginning when she was just a mistress to me. We had sex. We had fun. During that time Bryann was conceived. But shortly after I fell in love with her. She's not my mistress. She's my friend, my partner…"

"But not your wife," Kane broke into Kendall's poetic declaration. "If you love her so much then why are you still married to your wife? Come on, Son! Game recognize game. As men, we choose to be with the woman we want. There is no reason to stay with a woman you do not love."

"You say that because you don't have children," Kendall said. "People stay married for all sorts of reasons….least of all love."

"Damn, that is sad as hell," Kane said. He shook his head. "That is kind of what Farah said to me too. She stays with her husband for the sake of their family."

"Will you two please just SHUT THE HELL UP!!!" Riley stormed out of the room.

Kane looked at Kendall. "Am I tripping or is she crying?"

Kendall got up from the sofa, "Yep. That is the real Riley you see right there. I know she loves me. I love her. I wish I could change things."

"You can, dog. It's all your choice. You choose not to change it." Kane stood up and put his hand on Kendall's shoulder. "Let me ask you something… if both Lorraine and Riley were in this room and ran out crying at the same time. Who would you automatically go after to calm down? Quick! Without thinking…"

"Riley…" Kendall said quietly.

"Then, there is your answer."

"Answer to what?" Kendall asked.

"The answer to the question that you've been afraid to ask yourself all these years."

Kendall nodded his head slowly up and down. "Thanks man. That's real."

-4-

When Liv arrived at that park she looked around to see if she could figure out which car belonged to Dylan. There was a black Range Rover with gold trim package parked in the back corner of the lot. She pulled to the back of the lot and saw the "Alpha Phi Alpha" license plate frame. She caught herself smiling in the rear view mirror and quickly forced a frown and furrowed brow.

Liv jumped out of her car, took a deep breath and whispered to herself, "Olive Jones, you have moved on. The past is the past. Don't smile. Don't laugh and for God's sake do not let him kiss you."

She spotted Dylan. He sat alone on a bench under a tree. Liv felt her stomach churn the closer she got to him. She tried to deny those old feelings of fire and passion that brought them together years ago. He was the only man that ever made her break her marriage vows. He was also the reason she never took another lover. The broken heart Liv suffered trying to end her relationship with Dylan was enough to keep her from cheating on her husband ever again. It also caused her to gain a deeper relationship with her good friend, vodka.

Ironically, Dylan reminded Liv a lot of her husband, Adam. That was her initial attraction to him. Both men were pleasing to the eyes and heavy in the pockets. Dylan was handsome and smart and dressed like he was out of the pages of GQ magazine. Adam was fine and brilliant and dressed right off of fashion week runways. Both Dylan and Adam were very successful in their own right. Adam was a physician with a very successful practice. Dylan was a venture capitalist at Liv's last recollection.

"Hey you!" Liv said in a cheerful way, the way an older sister would approach her younger brother.

"Hey baby," Dylan said and stood to his feet.

Liv pulled back. "Dylan, please don't call me baby. Just call me Liv."

"I'm not calling you Liv, Olive. I've never called you that."

"Fine, then call me Olive. You can call me Sheila if you want to, but do not call me baby." She frowned to show him that she was seriously offended by his gesture.

He threw his hands up in surrender. "Okay, Okay Olive. I'm sorry to have offended you."

"Thank you." Liv sat down at the opposite end of the bench with about two feet between them.

Dylan chuckled and leaned back where he was seated before she arrived. He smiled and Liv felt the warmth on her face. Dylan was silent for a few moments. He looked at Liv as if he had been waiting to see her all of his life. He sighed. "Olive, I missed you."

"Thanks," Liv said without emotion.

"I thought of you every single day. There were so many times I wanted to pick up the phone and call you. But, I wanted to respect your wishes."

"Thank you," Liv said again.

Dylan nodded. "I want us to be friends Olive. We were so close. I miss you so much."

"Where's Hannah?"

"Hannah is gone," he said.

"Gone where Dylan? I've heard that a few times." Liv folded her arms. Her posture became defensive and cold.

"That's fair."

"Yes, it is. She leaves and comes back. Leaves and comes back. I am assuming she is still crazy." Liv frowned. She knew that was mean to say, but she had to keep her guard up with Dylan. One small crack and he could easily force his way back into her life and she knew it.

"She's not coming back, Olive. Hannah committed suicide."

Liv gasped. "Oh Dylan, I'm so sorry." She moved closer to him. "What happened? Oh gosh I'm sorry for being so mean about it."

"That's okay, baby…Uh…Olive. I know you are still hurt."

"No, I'm not still hurt Dylan. Not at all. I've moved on. Adam and I are doing really well. I have it all."

Dylan smiled, "I am glad you are happy." Liv opened her mouth to respond and Dylan interrupted her, "I know. I know. Thank you."

She smiled. "So how long has Hannah been…you know…gone."

"Three years."

"Three years? Wow! So what have you been doing with yourself?" Liv asked.

Dylan dipped his head and gave Liv a knowing look. "Trying to get up the nerve to come see you."

"Yeah right."

"It's true. I think about you all the time. When I saw you at that restaurant last week it was…"

She interrupted him. "…a coincidence. Nothing more."

Liv returned his knowing look. She was extremely guarded. She started to believe that she might actually be over Dylan. The initial butterflies she felt in her stomach were gone. She was quite comfortable sitting on the bench chatting with him. They were like two old friends catching up on all that has happened.

Dylan sold all the equity in his other ventures to start his own healthcare consulting firm. He was now in the business of buying up small medical practices and putting them into larger health systems to make them more profitable. From the looks of him, that venture was going very well. He looked and smelled like a million bucks.

"I really missed you Olive. Even at Hannah's funeral, I wanted you there to comfort me. I still love you very much," Dylan said.

Liv did not smile or blink for fear he would think she was batting her eyelashes at him. She said sternly, "I love Adam. I always have and I always will. What we had was a love affair, an escape from reality. That's all."

"You and I both know that is not true, Olive."

"Do we?" Liv asked with contempt in her voice. "So you think that after all this time you can waltz back into my life…my wonderful life…and sabotage it because your life has changed. So now that Hannah is gone I should drop everything and be with you. Is that what you think?"

Dylan kept silent for a moment. Then he nodded and simply said, "Yes."

"The nerve of you!" Liv shouted and turned her back to him.

"We had a plan to be together Olive. Remember?"

"Yes I remember, Dylan. A plan that I was all completely bought into and then you could not make the commitment to me. Now I have sons. It's the past."

"Olive, she was sick. If I had left her like that who knows what she would have done to herself. I had to stay." Dylan pleaded with his eyes.

Liv grabbed a flask from her bag and took a hard swig. She cleared her throat. "And how did that work out for you? Her sickness was not your problem or your fault. In the end there was nothing you could do and now…" she paused. "And now… I wish you the very best."

Liv turned her back again. There was a couple walking up the path towards them. She squinted. " Is that…"

"Well. Well. Well." Riley said as smug as she could possibly muster. "Look what I found. The faithful wife out here visiting with an old friend." She extended her hand towards Dylan. "It's nice to see you again Dylan."

Liv's face was nearly purple. She was unsure if she was jealous at Riley's flirting or if she was nervous because now she had given ammunition to the biggest troublemaker she knew. Riley created chaos everywhere she went. So this was sure to be something Liv and the girls would have to manage. If Adam found out that she met with Dylan he would never forgive her. All the years of hard work and rebuilding their love would be over. At the thought, Liv took another sip from her flask.

"There is good old American Express," Riley laughed referencing Liv's flask. "She doesn't leave home without it."

Both Dylan and Liv ignored Riley's insult. Dylan stood to his feet and stretched his hand to the man that was with Riley. "I'm sorry to be rude, man. I'm Dylan."

Riley stepped in between the two men. "There is no need for introductions. It's not likely you two will ever see each other again."

Dylan stepped around Riley. "Like I was saying…I'm Dylan. Nice to meet you."

Liv watched the man's expression. He was smiling from ear to ear. His smile put her in the mind of the wolf in Little Red Riding Hood. He was nearly salivating as he looked over at Riley before he offered up that knowing look to Dylan - the one men give each other when they know they are up to no good. Liv noticed the gold band around his finger. She shook her head as she watched Riley fawn all over Dylan.

"Dylan, why haven't you called me yet?" She asked.

Dylan cleared his throat. "It's good to meet you man. Good to see you Riley. You two love birds enjoy the day." He winked at the man.

Riley grabbed the man's hand in a huff and stomped off down the pathway. Liv was tickled because she had never seen Riley throw a tantrum. It was clear that Riley was used to getting her way, especially with men. The way Dylan dismissed her was a turn on for Liv. After a few shots of vodka and watching Dylan handle Riley, she had that old tingling feeling inside of her. She quickly came to her senses.

"I've got to go now," she said abruptly.

"Okay, I'll walk you to your car." Dylan stood and extended his hand.

Liv took his hand and stumbled a bit as she stood. She was not sure if it was the vodka or the clean smell of his cologne that nearly knocked her off her feet. She looked up at him and her mouth salivated as she thought of smooth, sweet milk chocolate. He really was darn near perfectly made. Her physical attraction to him was a strong as ever but she had moved on. Vodka or no vodka, Liv was unwilling to sacrifice her happy life for a trip to the past. It was gone. She and Dylan had no present and no future.

"Ugh, I sound like Callie," she accidentally said aloud.

"Pardon?" Dylan asked politely.

"Oh, nothing. I was just thinking about something."

"Callie….you said you sound like Callista." He inquired. "What does that mean?"

Liv sighed. "You know I am a hopeless romantic and Callie is always telling me to be realistic. Now I'm telling myself that very thing. This is not a fairytale. You did not come back after all these years to sweep me away to a happily ever after. This is real life Dylan. What we thought we had is over. Gone."

"Really?" he asked before bending down with an open mouth and kissing Liv like she had not been kissed since the day they parted ways.

His lips tasted like green apple and watermelon. The kiss was sweet but sour and made her mouth water. Her panties were just about as wet as her tongue and she finally gave in and melted into his arms. He squeezed her tight. The passion was still there. The intense attraction was still there. She wrapped herself in his scent as they continued to explore with their tongues swirling. They kissed as if they were inside closed doors. To Liv, it felt like they were the only two people God ever created on the planet. She had forgotten her husband, her children, her parents, and her friends. There was just Dylan and her.

As they continued to kiss and rub each other, Dylan led her to his truck. "Get in."

Surprisingly Liv's body moved on his command. She climbed into the truck and he shut the door gently while keeping eye contact with her. She watched in the rear view mirror as he calmly walked around the car. He seemed to glide. When he got into his seat he leaned over again and kissed Liv with that sweetly sour taste of secret love. She thought they were going to just sit in the car and make out for a while, but Dylan put his keys in the ignition and drove off down the street.

"Where are we going?" She asked.

Before there was even enough time to answer they pulled up at a small boutique hotel down the block from the park. She looked at him. He looked at her. Everything in her mind wanted to shout "No". Everything in her body shouted "yes" including her heart. How could she do this to Adam again? Liv was disgusted in herself, yet unable to keep the passion from flowing through her. This feeling was all she ever wanted. It was the very feeling she dreamed of as a little girl. It was the feeling that Hollywood tried to portray so that we all feel so terrible about our practical, every day mundane love.

Dylan walked around and opened her door for her. She took a quick sip from her flask and dropped it back in her purse. She did not need liquid courage. She needed something to calm her down because she could have taken off all of her clothes right in the parking lot. Liv was so hot for Dylan and she missed the fire they had together. He led her through the lobby of the hotel and then pushed the elevator button. When the doors opened the empty elevator triggered memories for Liv of times when she and Dylan made passionate love behind closed elevator doors. Dylan let her walk in first and she leaned again the back wall smiling like a teenage girl. He pushed the sixth floor button. Suddenly it dawned on her.

"Wait! You already had a room?"

Dylan smiled at her.

"Are you freaking kidding me?" She pushed herself past him and hit the button so the elevator would stop at the next floor. When the doors opened she jumped off the elevator. "What an idiot! I am so stupid."

"What are you talking about Olive?" Dylan stood holding the door.

"Goodbye Dylan." Liv pushed the down button to call another elevator to her rescue.

"Wait. Let's talk about this." He said.

"Talk about what? You planned this. You got a hotel room knowing you would break me down. Do not ever contact me again."

"Okay, just let me take you back to your car and we can talk about this."

"I'll walk. It's only a block and a half." Liv said. She climbed onto an arriving elevator and went down to the lobby.

As she pushed through the front doors of the hotel, Dylan came running after her. She walked faster across the parking lot to make her way down the sidewalk and back to her car. He followed. She heard his footsteps get faster behind her. Was he running? She turned around and, yes, he was running after her. She smiled before catching herself. She screamed back to him, "Leave me alone Dylan. Go away."

Dylan quickly caught up to her. "Just wait. I am sorry to be presumptuous. It wasn't meant to be like that. I was just very excited to be reunited with you, Olive. I promise."

Liv kept stomping down the sidewalk. Her car was in view. Dylan paced beside her every step of the way and tried to explain himself. People driving by had begun to stare at the two of them. It was clear that this was lover's quarrel. It made for good reality TV and even better reality. Cars slowed down and watched as they drove by the way they do when there is a bad accident on the road.

"You are making a scene," Liv said.

"No, I'm making a case. Will you just listen to me?"

"No!" Liv shouted. "You made a fool of me."

"How?" Dylan asked.

"You think you can just come after all these years and get right in my pants, huh?"

"It's not like that," Dylan explained. "I've been dreaming of this day for so long. I know our passion is still there. I know you still love me."

"No I do not. I love your kiss. I love your smell and I love MY HUSBAND!"

"I don't believe that." Dylan said firmly.

"Well, I guess I'll just have to make you a believer." With that, Liv got in her car and drove away with Dylan standing in the parking lot. There was a group of mothers and their young children on the playground. They watched intently with sad eyes as if watching a Lifetime movie.

Liv sped out onto the street. The tears she had been fighting to hold back finally flowed from her eyes. Keeping her eyes on the road she fumbled through her purse to find her flask. Opening it with her teeth she twisted off the cap and poured the rest of the vodka down her throat as tears poured down her face. "Callie was right. Love is just a waiting room for heartache."

-5-

Greg's cologne filled the car and Farah was delighted to be seeped in his scent. She was unsure of how she was going to make it through the night with Greg's mother Eva, but she would try for Greg's sake. He had not told his parents that they were separated and Farah felt strange keeping the secret from them. However, she totally understood why Greg made the decision to keep their problems away from his mother.

"I'm glad Liv and Callie will be with me tonight," Farah sighed.

"Yeah, I'm surprised Acer was cool with Callie coming. I guess they are over each other."

"Please! They have been over each other. Those two are so much alike. They care for themselves too much to even consider pining away for someone else," Farah said.

Greg nodded, "That's true. But how nice would it be if they had stayed together."

"I know." Farah thought about it. Callie would have been her sister-in-law and her best friend. "But I love Callie too much to wish your mother upon her." Farah laughed.

Greg chuckled, "Yeah, but she's white so my mom would have loved her on principle."

"True. True." Farah laughed.

The two of them had made the best of his mother's opposition to their marriage. Farah had endured quite a bit of tongue in cheek racism from her mother-in-law over the years. Greg had many arguments with his mother about his love for Farah. He made it clear to Eva that he loved Farah and that she would be his wife. Eventually, Eva had to accept Farah in order not to lose the relationship with her son.

Farah's stomach started to swirl as soon as they drove through the front gates. Adam and Liv followed behind them. Both couples jumped out of their cars and Greg grabbed Farah's hand. Liv took a swig from her flask before stashing it away in her MK clutch bag. Farah looked at her.

"What?" Liv asked. "You do not think I can be around this woman sober, do you?"

"There will be plenty to drink inside," Farah said. "Must you bring that flask everywhere we go?"

"Yes!" Liv said with conviction. "Before I get inside to the bar I will have to face the evil queen," she said with a curtsey.

"Well on that note, pass the Courvoisier!" Farah snapped. She and Liv cracked up in laughter.

"I'm standing right here. I can hear you two talking about my mother," Greg said with a smile. "So be sure to save a shot for me," he joked.

They all sauntered up the brick walkway leading to the house. Everyone stepped slowly as if prolonging the inevitable. Greg squeezed Farah's hand as he rang the doorbell. "I love you," he said with an appreciative grin. "Thank you for doing this with me."

Farah blew him a kiss in response.

Eva opened the door and the smell of Chanel #5 caused Farah to wince. Greg coughed, "Good Lord, Mom. You have on too much perfume. And that skirt is kind of short, isn't it?"

 Eva ignored Greg's remark and looked over at Farah. "Hello, dear. How wonderful to see you," Eva snarled. Farah despised the way her mother-in-law pronounced "wunda-ful". Every time she said it, sarcasm slid like snot from her nose.

Eva's face looked like saltwater taffy pulled around a jack-o-lantern. This was, of course, due to the pile of plastic surgery receipts tucked away in the attic. Eva Goodwyn was getting her nips, tucks and fills long before women found the need to trade aging gracefully for conspicuously remaining young. Her nostrils were no longer round, but the shape of half moon crescents. As if she wanted a way to show her snobbery without effort, her nose pointed upward into a flat square tip at the end. The doctors had tinkered with her eyes, nose, lips, neck, and the corners of her mouth. Eva was authentically phony from her clip in ponytail down to the press on toenails.

"Oh Farah, darling. Why don't you ever show off those ethnic curves of yours? You stay covered like one of those terrorist women."

"Come here mom. You need a hug." Greg lifted his mother's thin frame slightly above the ground. Eva glanced over Greg's shoulder at Farah as if it were some kind of victory that she received a hug from her son. A smile stretched across Eva's face like the joker…Ledger not Nicholson.

Thankfully, Greg's father came to the door. Judge Goodwyn looked like an older, more seasoned version of JFK. Farah imagined that if JFK had lived longer, he would look exactly like Judge Goodwyn. He was extremely handsome and distinguished in a classic way that never fades. He had the perfect genetic makeup to neutralize Eva's hardened features. Though he was purely Anglo Saxon, Charles Goodwyn had dark features that could be easily mistaken for Greek or Italian. It was those piercing dark features that first attracted Farah to Greg. Thank goodness Greg looked nothing like his mother and strongly resembled his father's handsome traits.

"Eva, allow them in the door please." Judge Goodwyn reached around his wife to give Greg a hug and he kissed Farah on the cheek. Then he extended a hand toward Adam, "Dr. Jones, I'm glad you could come. I may have you look at my ticker while you're here. I've been a bit winded lately on the tennis court."

"No problem Judge Goodwyn," Adam said. "You did buy my very first stethoscope."

"That's right," Judge Goodwyn laughed with a nod. "I remember that."

Adam nodded. "Yep, and Dad bought the cash register that turned Greg into the greedy bastard he is today." Adam threw an elbow in Greg's side with a chuckle.

Charles Goodwyn had a huge smile on his face. "Yes, I remember the day. I sure miss my buddy. God rest the dead."

Adam dropped his head. Eva rolled her eyes. Her husband's "bleeding liberal heart" had always annoyed her. When Adam's parents moved a few houses down in the 1970's they integrated the neighborhood. The neighbors were in an uproar until Judge Goodwyn stepped forward and stopped all the nonsense. He truly believed in what America was supposed to stand for…liberty and justice for ALL.

The men peeled off to the study to have their secret toast of thirty-year-old scotch that Judge Goodwyn kept for family use only. The girls entered the formal dining room that had been cleared out for mingling and cocktails. Farah was surprised to see that Callie had already arrived. "Hey! What are you doing here? I didn't see your car."

"Well, I figured I might be in no shape to drive and one of you guys can take me home. I know you drove two cars," she said with a wink.

Callie was right. Liv and Farah always insisted on driving two cars whenever they all went out together in case the girls needed to leave the guys behind for emergency estrogen therapy. In Farah's opinion, this was sure to be one of those times.

Callie continued, "So I had someone drop me off a little while ago."

Liv repeated with a grin, "Someone."

"Exactly," Farah said and gave her friend a big hug. "Well, I'm glad 'someone' could bring you."

Callie grabbed a glass of champagne from the bar tray and Liv had the bartender give her an empty champagne flute from behind the bar. "

"She hired a full staff?" Liv whispered.

Farah rolled her eyes. "We are talking about Eva, right?"

"And for you madam?" the bartender asked Farah.

"Oh, I'll have a pomegranate cosmopolitan and make it a double," she said.

Callie frowned. "Still drinking, Huh? I guess you've just given up on sobriety."

"That's a good idea!" Liv perked and emptied her flask into the champagne glass. "Leave her alone, Callie. There are times to be sober and this is not one of them." She tossed the empty flask in her bag and posed with her pinky in the air. "Look how cute I am."

The three ladies walked out into the garden where they saw Greg's younger brother. Acer, who never really made a connection to adult life, still lived at home with his parents and spent all his money on old cars and new women. He was Eva's favorite son without question. One of the beautiful people, he made his way around the garden party chuckling with the men and winking at the women.

"And there he is… the man of my dreams." Callie shouted across the yard. "I'm still so in love with you," she swooned.

Liv leaned in to Farah and whispered with air quotes, "And now we know why 'someone' dropped her off."

"Yup! Exactly!" Farah nodded. "I knew from the moment I saw her in that white dress. All wrapped around that tiny waist and tight booty."

Callie spoke through perfect clenched teeth aimed at Acer who was now approaching. "I can hear you girls."

"Ahhhh, beautiful Callista, the love of my life." Acer kissed the back of Callie's hand. "When are you going to marry me?"

"That would be never," Callie said sweetly. She put her hand on her heart and let out a dramatic sigh.

Acer and Callie had a long history together…almost sixteen years at this point. They met when Greg and Farah were planning the wedding. It was all quite cliché. Callie was the Maid of Honor and Acer was the Best Man. They dated for little while after the wedding but Callie wanted more than Acer could give her at the time…truth and fidelity. Shortly after she fell madly in love with the next guy.

After the death of her fiancé when Callie turned victim-vixen, she hooked back up with Acer and gave him a taste of his own medicine. He quickly fell back in love with her but still could not be faithful and though she "felt something" she had no intention of being in a relationship ever again. So, they continued this pattern of "checking up on it" a couple times a year.

"You know you are going to be my wife one day, don't you?" Acer moved in close to Callie, nose to nose.

She smiled, never losing eye contact with Acer. "I do," she said mimicking marital vows.

"Oh please! The two of you are making me nauseous," Liv said.

"Me, too." Farah pretended to gag. "Get on with it already."

"Not me," Adam said. He came up from behind and wrapped his arms around Liv. "I know how intoxicating love can be."

Unlike Callie and Acer, Adam was not being sarcastic. "I love Olive Jones and all I want in life is to keep her happy. Isn't that right, baby?" He kissed Liv on the back of her head.

Liv had given him four beautiful sons in a perfectly ordered and gender-biased household. It was just like the home where he was raised. The boys run rough-shot over the caregivers while Liv sips martinis, shops, and attaches her name to a few charities. Adam brought home the money and Liv spent it on herself and the kids…in that order. He loved it. She knew to appreciate it. So instead of complaining about her lack of self-fulfillment, she numbed herself with liquor and took on the superficial alter ego as a spoiled, highly maintained housewife.

Liv turned and kissed her husband. "Sweetheart will you get me a dirty martini please?" She handed him the empty champagne flute that disguised her vodka. When Adam walked back inside to the bar Liv pulled Callie away from Acer and grabbed Farah's hand. Her face was red, but not the usual alcoholic flush faced. Something else was going on so Farah became concerned.

"I need to talk to you guys," Liv said.

"What's wrong?" Farah asked with more professional concern than BFF care.

Callie still kept her attention on Acer. She blew him a kiss before turning back to Liv. "This better be good because I passed up on a night with 'someone' to be here in support of Farah. My consolation prize is a night with Acer. So hurry it up!"

"Okay. Okay." Liv looked back toward the doorway to the house to make sure Adam was not coming back out to her. "I met with Dylan."

"What!" Farah and Callie squealed at once.

"When?" Farah asked.

"Where?" Callie questioned.

"Why?" They said in unison loudly.

"Shhhh, stop drawing attention to us," Liv scolded.

"There are three hundred white people staring at Eva's black daughter-in-law. Our voices are not the spectacle drawing attention to us." Callie said.

"Gee thanks for keeping it real," Farah quipped.

"No problem," Callie responded, but totally missing Farah's sarcasm.

"We'll talk about it later," Liv whispered and looked back at the door once again.

"What? I can barely hear you over this horrible band playing their 'whites only' jazz," Callie said with a grin.

"This place is ridiculous. It's the whitest place I've ever been in my life. I mean…and I'm white."

"Excuse me, ladies." Acer crept up behind Callie and pulled her away. "You ladies get her all the time. She's mine tonight."

Farah frowned at Liv and saw Adam entering the garden. "He's coming back. We'll talk about this later."

Adam handed Liv her dirty martini and had also gotten Farah another cosmo. No sooner than Farah placed her first glass down on the high top table, a young Hispanic woman in a maid's uniform came running over to retrieve the glass as if she appeared out of thin air.

"Damn! Ninja maid!" Liv grimaced.

"Girl, you know Eva does not play around with the help. In her mind she believes she is a plantation mistress during these parties." Farah shook her head. "Thanks favorite neighbor," Farah said to Adam thanking him for the refill.

"Just don't tell Greg I got it for you," he said with a frown. "He's worried about your drinking."

"I have it under control, Adam." Farah lifted her glass in an air toast.

Adam smiled at her but his eyes said he was worried about her too. "Looks like Callie and Acer are back at it again." He shifted the subject.

"Yep," Liv said and drank nearly half of her martini in one gulp.

"Slow down, honey." Adam kissed her cheek. "We have a long night ahead of us." He nodded toward Eva and another woman walking toward them. Farah quickly took a sip of her drink.

"Farah darling," she snarled, "Meet my friend Patti. Her husband has a new black boss and she wants to have him over for dinner. Can you tell her how to make fried chicken and those..ummm.. colored greens?" Eva turned toward her friend and lowered her voice. "She can help. Her family hails from Harlem."

"Oh thank you!" Patti said. "I usually make steak and asparagus but I know your people don't eat asparagus and you are very fond of chicken."

Farah looked at Adam and Liv. She looked back at her mother-in-law, then up to the sky. She calmly took a sip of her cosmo followed by a deep breath. Then, she politely smiled and walked away from her mother-in-law.

"It's collard…" Adam corrected. "It's not colored greens. It's collard greens."

"Oh Adam you are so articulate," Eva said before moving on in the crowd.

Once Eva walked away, Farah approached Adam and Liv again. This time she had Riley beside her. "You guys remember Riley."

"Hey," Liv said half-heartedly. Adam greeted Riley with a customary kiss on the cheek. Though Farah and Liv both braced themselves for something completely inappropriate from her, Riley simply said hello.

When Callie saw Riley from across the yard she dashed over to the group. "Ummmm, what is she doing here?" she asked Farah.

"She's here to meet everyone. Riley is apart of our family now."

Riley cleared her throat. "Hello Callista."

Callie looked Riley up and down. Surprising, Riley was dressed appropriately for the occasion. Her clothes were fitted, but not too tight. Her cleavage was enough to garner praise without a lot of attention and she had matched a purple pencil skirt very well with a tasteful, sleeveless silk blouse. Callie was annoyed, but secretly impressed with Riley's ability to tone down her usual in-your-face sexuality.

"Hello Riley." Callie extended her hand.

Riley folded her arms.

"Glad to see we are still on the same page," Callie said. She shrugged and walked back over to Acer.

Riley watched as Callie strutted across the garden Liv noticed the envy stretched across Riley's face. It was clear that Riley was used to being the center of attention, the absolute hottie of every room she entered.

"Callie is wearing that dress," Liv said.

"She sure is," Farah said, not knowing that Liv had made the statement for Riley's benefit.

Riley tilted her head to the side, "Eh, she's a little hippy for a white girl." She turned around, "What do you think Adam? How does Callie's butt look in that dress?"

Liv frowned and her eyes squinted in hostility.

"Never mind, you better not answer that," Riley chuckled.

Riley was no dummy. She knew exactly what Liv was doing. Riley had a moment of envy towards Callie but quickly came to her senses. She knew that if she had dressed in her customary attire, nobody would take a second glance at Callie in that tight white dress and those red "give it to me good" high heels.

She watched Callie and Acer from across the garden. "Who's that guy with Callie? He's cute."

"Oh, that's Acer. Greg's younger brother." Farah watched Riley's eyes dance.

"Is he married?" Riley asked.

"Nope," Farah answered reluctantly.

"Hmmmm," Riley smiled. "What's up with he and Callista?"

Liv swigged the end of her martini, "Oh they go way back." Farah frowned at Liv but the level of vodka in her system made her miss the cue. "One year they are in love. The next they are not. They will eventually get married."

"Is that so? It's that serious, huh?" Riley asked with a coy grin.

"It's THAT serious," Liv said as she and Riley both gazed at Acer and Callie ogling each other.

"Hmph," Riley twisted her lips. "Interesting."

Farah was uncomfortable with the brightness shining across Riley's flawless features. She was up to something. "Riley…listen…we are trying to build our family. Callie is apart of that. She and Bryann are very close. You need to get along with her. She's Bryann's aunt."

"And I'm Bryann's mother." Riley sashayed down the walk towards Callie and Acer. She walked right up into the group and extended her hand to Acer. "Hello, I'm Riley Briggs."

Acer's eyes bulged to the size of golf balls. He looked down at her feet and back up again. "Hello…I'm Acer Goodwyn."

Callie let out a long sigh. "Yes, Riley is Bryann's birthmother."

"She's what!" Acer raised his voice louder than socially acceptable. "I had no idea."

"That your niece was adopted?" Riley asked with a victorious grin.

"No…" Acer frowned. "That her birthmother would be here…at our family gathering." He grabbed Callie's hand. "What is Farah thinking," he whispered to Callie.

Callie shrugged, "You know your sister-in-law. She didn't have a family and she's very serious about making sure Bryann has the best family memories."

"Not very smart..." Acer said.

"I agree," Callie responded with a kiss to Acer and a wicked glance to Riley. She grabbed Riley's hand and pulled with just enough force to send a message to Riley that Acer was off limits. "Come on, let's go hang with the girls."

Acer excused himself, motioned for Adam to follow him. They walked inside to find Greg holding court with potential clients in the living room. "Excuse me big brother, can I talk to you for a second?"

"Uh, sure." Greg looked perplexed and excused himself.

"I just met Bryann's birthmother!" Acer said. He looked both frightened and angry at the same time. "Why would Farah invite her into our family?"

"You know Farah..."

"Yeah, Yeah... Callie said the same thing. I know Farah. No family. Sad story. Boohoo!" Acer growled.

"Hey! Hold on there little brother. What's wrong with you?" Greg asked.

Adam put his hand on Greg's shoulder in support.

"I'll tell you what's wrong with me. I love my family." Acer drew in near to his brother and Adam. "And I love Callista."

"Okay…." Greg and Adam said at once.

"So…" Greg said.

"So? So!" Acer leaned in closer and whispered, "So I've been sexing her for over a month…regularly…with great ambition I might add. I get it every chance I get because it's so good."

"Callie?" Adam asked.

"No. Riley," Acer whispered. "Why didn't you tell the name of Bryann's birth mother?"

"What!!!" Greg shouted a cluster of people looked over toward the group.

"Oh I am out of here. I want no part of this conversation…" Adam mumbled.

"Don't move…" Acer said. "You are in this, too."

"How am I in this?" Adam asked.

Greg looked at Adam, "Because…when the girls find out about this we are all in for a lot of painful days."

"We? You don't even live with your wife…" Adam whispered.

"What?" Acer shouted. Again…drawing attention to the group. "You and Farah are separated? When did this happen. Oh God, mom is going to throw a party."

"Don't you say a word to her. We are working it out so keep it to yourself. Do you hear me?" Greg commanded of his younger brother.

"Don't worry. I want to stay far away from this one." Acer said holding his forehead in his hands.

"And you better stay far away from that other one too…" Greg nodded his head toward the doorway as Farah, Liv, Callie, and Riley walked through like runway models during Mercedes Benz Fashion week.

"They are all so fine though…" Adam said.

Greg and Acer both frowned at Adam.

"What? Don't be mad at me," he said, "You two need to take lessons from the master."

As Liv approached Adam leaned in and kissed her on the cheek. Then he winked at his boys.

-6-

Farah and Greg sat in the driveway of what used to be their perfect home. She felt obligated to invite him in but she was not sure that he would say yes. Farah wanted her husband back at home with Bryann and her.

"So thanks for doing that with me, " Greg said. "I know it was not easy for you."

"It is our family." Farah smiled at her estranged husband.

He chuckled. "I don't think I've ever heard you call my mother your family. That's new."

"There are a lot of new things happening with me," Farah said.

"Yes, like drinking." Greg pursed his lips together and stared at Farah.

"I know Greg. I know. I'm going to get back on the wagon. I promise." She paused for a moment. "Wow! Spoken like a true alcoholic."

"Yep," Greg said. "When? When Farah? When will you get sober again? All of those years just washed away because of a decision you made to take an affair too far."

Puzzled, Farah looked at him. "Excuse me?"

"Your relationship with Kane Taylor took away your sobriety."

"No! My guilt over Kane Taylor rocked my sobriety. " She turned towards him. "I told you Greg. It's over."

"Yes. A little too late," he said before turning off the ignition. "I'll walk you to the door."

"I can manage," Farah said. Now she was starting to get angry. She thought they had a great night and was sure that this would get them on the road to reconciliation. But it seemed that Greg still harbored a lot of resentment.

Before getting out of the car. Farah turned back towards Greg. "You are the best thing that ever happened to me."

"I know," he said. "And you are the best thing to ever happen to me."

"So then what happened to us?" Farah asked.

"You did," he replied angrily. Greg nodded goodnight and looked straight ahead waiting for Farah to get out of the car.

"I guess that is true." Farah gave a sheepish smile and got out of the car. "Goodnight Greg."

"Goodnight Farah. I love you," he said without looking in her direction.

Farah went into the empty house and kicked off her shoes. She headed straight to the kitchen and pulled the bottle of vodka from under the cabinet. It was about half empty…or half full depending on what mood Farah was in that day. This evening, the bottle was half full and offering her some desperately needed comfort.

She pulled her arms around and unzipped her dress as far as she could before slipping out of her bra from underneath. "Aaaahhh much better."

Opening the freezer she tossed two small cubes of ice in her glass and slowly poured the vodka over top of it. As she poured Farah felt excited. She felt relaxed. She felt love. She had rekindled her relationship with vodka and it made her feel so good. She watched as the clear liquid folded over the ice and slid down into the glass. She imagined it would slide down her throat the same way. She smiled and caught a glimpse of herself in the window above the sink.

It was at that moment she knew it was way past time to call her sponsor. So she stood there for a moment in thought. Farah could empty the glass and half-full bottle into the sink. She held the glass up and looked at it. The rush she felt was a keen reminder that she was, without question, an alcoholic. She decided that she would call Nenah, her sponsor and coach.

Farah took the half-full bottle and emptied it into the sink. Pain rushed through her body as the vodka swirled down the drain. The she lifted the glass and drank it in one gulp as if it were the last hurrah.

She dialed Nenah's number and it rang only once before there was a voice on the other end.

"Farah?"

"Hey, did I wake you?"

"No," Nenah said in a groggy and startled voice that explained just how deep asleep she was before the call.

"Yes, I did," Farah said.

"Farah, what's going on? I'm glad you finally called."

"Finally?" Farah asked.

"Yes, Greg called some time ago and told me you were in trouble."

"He did what?" Farah questioned with attitude. "He had no right to do that. What's the point in being 'anonymous' if he can just call you up and squeal?"

Nenah sighed and Farah could hear her adjusting her position as the phone rustled. Perhaps now she was sitting up in the bed, which meant she was in work mode…therapy. "He had every right to do so as your husband. You know that your drinking does not only impact you. It impacts your whole family – everyone who loves you."

Farah jumped up on the kitchen counter to sit. She looked over and noticed that Bryann had left one pecan chocolate chip cookie in the package so she grabbed it and popped it in her mouth.

With a mouth full of cooked, Farah grumbled, "Can we do this tomorrow?"

"No, right now." Nenah insisted.

"Okay fine…" Farah rolled her eyes and shook her head.

"Farah, why are you drinking again?"

"Because my world has been turned upside down. Riley Briggs came into my life like a raging volcano."

Nenah responded, "Uh hu…and what did she do."

"What did she do?" Farah exclaimed. "Well, first she destroyed my family, my marriage and my life."

"…and how did she do that?" Nenah asked.

"She made us tell Bryann she was adopted. She made me fall in love with Kane and she sent pictures to Greg of me and Kane."

Nenah remained quiet. She wanted to give Farah an opportunity to assess those words. Farah was a phenomenal psychiatrist and Nenah respected her very much. Nenah only provided Farah guidance to bring awareness to what she already knows.

Farah broke the silence, "Well in all of that the only things she really did was send the pictures. It wasn't Riley's fault we kept the adoption a secret and she certainly did not force me into a relationship with Kane… "

"Mmhm." Nenah affirmed.

"I guess I am responsible for my broken sobriety, not Riley. She was simply the trigger."

"Yes, she was."

"The truth is I am an alcoholic with many years of sobriety under my belt. I've got to start all over again," Farah moaned.

"Yes you do," Nenah agreed. She paused. "Farah…do you remember why you started drinking in the first place. I'm not talking about this time, but in the very beginning. When did your problems start?"

"At birth!" Farah joked with a chuckle. "My problems all started the day I was born to my mother and to a man whom I do not know anything about. My drinking problems started shortly after Greg and I were married."

"And what was the trigger?" Nenah asked.

"Loneliness? I guess."

"You guess…" Nenah's smile came through the phone and made Farah smile.

"Well, after I married Greg and we got Bryann I realized all that I had missed out on in life. Losing my mother before I could even remember her and having no clue who my father is left a gaping hole in who I am as a person."

"Mmhmm…" Nenah agreed. "And that hole is still there. You can't fill it with alcohol, work, or sex with strange men."

Farah thought for a moment. She knew that Nenah was right. She had always known that she was trying to dull her pain with sex in place of alcohol during her sobriety.

"You know. I think I just realized something…" Farah said.

"What's that?"

"I stopped drinking but I was still an addict. I just replaced alcohol with work and when work got easy I replaced it with sex."

"Yes, Dr. Goodwyn…and I am 100% positive this is not the moment you realized that." Nenah smiled again through the phone.

Farah laughed a bit, "I suppose you are right Dr. Desi."

"So what created that hole?" Nenah asked.

"My parents." Farah knew exactly what she was missing in life.

"And how can you fill that hole now?"

Farah thought for a moment, "Well, my mother is dead and there is nothing I can do about that…."

"Mmm hmmm," Nenah agreed.

"But I'm not sure about my father. Who he is? Is he still alive?" Farah wondered aloud.

Nenah listened to Farah think out loud before offering advice. "Farah, there is a new site that is proving to be very successful. It's called 'Out Here' and it is a match site for adopted and orphaned children. Really it is for anyone who has been separated from family and wants to find relatives – distant and close. You should try it."

"I'm not so sure I want to do that," Farah said.

"Okay, well just think about it." Nenah said. "One last thing Farah…I have to ask this and you know why."

"Yes…" Farah sighed. "Here it comes."

"Yep," Nenah cleared her throat. "How did your mother die?"

Farah's shoulders slumped in defeat. She knew that it was her sponsor's job to get her re-centered and to keep her in the reality of what alcoholism does to families.

Farah sighed and spoke inside of a long exhale. "She was drunk. I was just a baby in my car seat. She and my aunt had gotten into an argument and my mother put me in the car and drove away. She ran off the road. God spared my life but not hers." Farah continued with what has been a clearly rehearsed statement of fact and conviction. "I was then raised by my Aunt Janice who did not give me the love and care I desired. It caused me to make choices that were not necessarily what I really wanted but what I felt I needed to get through life. Alcoholism caused the car wreck that killed my mother when I was just a baby and it set the spark for the events in my life. My decision to continue drinking alcohol will continue the momentum of destruction that I have battled since the day I was born."

"Good job, Farah." Nenah let out a pleasing sigh, "I remember when you would be sobbing in tears at the end of that."

"Yep, me too."

"I'm proud of you, Farah," Nenah said.

Well, tomorrow is day one." Farah put the empty glass in the sink and went upstairs to bed.

-7-

"Good morning beautiful. How are we going to spend our day?"

Callie shot up in the bed. "Oh damn! What are you doing here?"

Acer laughed, "Well, you know you didn't have your car with you last night so somebody had to take you home."

Callie thought back to her conversation with Farah and Liv last night. "Somebody" keeps getting her in trouble. She smiled about that. If she could not find love she definitely enjoyed finding trouble with "somebody".

"So why didn't one of the girls take me home?" Callie asked.

"Because I offered," Acer said with a kiss to the tip of Callie's nose.

"Of course you did." She twisted her lips. Callie looked over on the nightstand and there were two aspirin and a bottle for Gatorade. She turned toward Acer.

He smiled, "I know my girl."

She grabbed the aspirin popped them in her mouth and took a swig of the Gatorade. "Ahhh thank you. I must have had five glasses of champagne last night."

"Seven, but nobody was counting," Acer smiled.

"Ugh, I bet your mother was counting."

"My mother pays no attention to you. She's too busy focused on Farah's flaws."

"What flaws? What's the deal with that anyway? After all these years, why can't your mother accept that Greg loves Farah?"

Acer contorted his face as if Callie spoke another language. "Umm because she's Black. You do know my mother is a closet racist?"

Callie responded, "Ummm no. Your mother is a flat out racist. If she's in the closet, the door is made of plexiglass."

"Be nice about my mother." Acer said, trying to be stern.

Callie let out a burst of laughter. "Please. Even you aren't nice to your mother."

"Let's talk about us," he said changing the subject. "We are in bed together. We had an amazing night last night. Now what?"

"Ugh," Callie mocked. "You are still such a girl…"

"And you are still such a dude. It's okay to have emotions. I know you love me."

Callie twisted her lips. "You're joking right? Just because I put your penis in my mouth does not mean that you have gained some magical control over my mind and emotions." She shook her head. "Men!"

"What about us?" Acer asked.

"You really think sex changes a woman's emotions? Sex changes how you guys feel, not us."

"You are barking up the wrong tree with that one because you know women fall in love with me after just one stroke."

Callie rolled her eyes, "This is why you still live at home."

"There is no reason for me to have a mortgage when I spend six nights a week in the bed with a beautiful woman somewhere else." Acer inhaled in victory.

"Just six?" Callie mocked.

"Well, even God rested on the seventh."

"You are a piece of work, Acer Goodwyn. Get out of my bed."

"Nope," he said.

"Nope?"

"Yeah. Nope." Acer locked eyes with Callie. "We are going to deal with whatever this is that has been going on between us for the last decade."

"You can deal with whatever you want, but I am getting up and going about my day. I'm going over to spend time with Bryann today – without her wicked step mother."

"Wicked step mother?"

"Yeah, Riley…" Callie's anger spread across her face. "That woman!"

Acer took a hard swallow. "Yeah, she seems like she's trouble."

"I mean…" Callie sat up in the bed, " She comes from out of nowhere to wreck a perfectly happy family…one of the happiest families I've ever seen."

Acer held up one hand. "Wait a minute. Farah and Greg had plenty of problems before Riley. And although I'd never say it to Farah…she didn't have to take the bait with Kane Taylor. Riley sent him in to seduce her. She fell into his bed all on her own."

"She fell more than into his bed. She fell in love." Callie shook her head.

"I don't believe that," Acer said. "She and my brother love each other. They have fought to be together all of these years. Between my mother and Farah's Aunt Janice it is a miracle they even got married."

"Aunt Janice loved Greg. He's white and she loved white men."

"So do you…" Acer bit Callie on the neck.

"Stop. This is serious. Get back on your side." Callie pushed him away from her.

He smiled, "Oh I have a side."

"You know what I mean Acer. Cut it out."

"You want me here with you don't you."

"Acer, what we had was a long time ago. We tried it twice. It didn't work."

"Let's try it again," he said. His eyes were dark and piercing. He was serious.

Callie leaned in toward his lips. She kept her eyes locked on his. Slowly she opened her mouth and swirled her tongue. He moved in closer to her and let out a sigh.

"Uh NO!" Callie said. "Are you nuts? This was one night and one night too many."

"Callie, you know we were meant to be together."

"Yes, as godparents to our goddaughter."

"Nope. As more." Acer declined. "Besides it is silly for me to be Bryann's uncle and godfather. Farah and Greg only did that so we would be together." He nestled in again. "So let's give them what they want.

Callie rolled her eyes. "Get out of my bed."

-8-

"I had sex with Acer last night," Callie tossed her news right out into the middle of greeting the girls like a grenade.

"You had sex with WHO?" Liv chuckled.

"Well we could have seen that coming," Farah remarked with a smirk. "I knew last night was going to bring back old feelings between you two."

"What old feelings?" Callie asked and folded her arms.

"Oh, I forgot you do not have feelings, Detective Piper," Farah said.

Callie grinned, "Not above my waist."

Farah's eyes widened. "Shhh here comes Bryann. I don't need her hearing about her godparents in bed. Geesh!"

"Too late. I already know," Bryann entered the room looking like an average 15-year-old girl. "I heard grandma say that Uncle Acer took Aunt Callie home last night and we all know what that means." She kissed her aunts on the cheek.

Her hair had obviously been pulled back into a high ponytail without using a brush. To Farah's pleasure, Bryann was not wearing make-up and she had two small silver hoops in her ears. Though it was technically spring, teenagers could still get away with wearing Uggs and fleeces for fashion purposes. Bryann modeled her brand new pair of $160 jeans looked dirty and 160 years old.

They are "New Vintage," she boasted.

 "Who pays that much money for jeans that look like that?" Callie asked her goddaughter.

"I do…" Bryan replied, "I mean technically she does." She pointed at her mother.

Liv entered the conversation, "Well, you look cute in them."

"Thanks! I feel great." Bryann shined a bright smile. "I'm doing so well. Huh Mom?"

"Yes, you are sweetheart." Farah gave her a side hug and Bryann placed her head on her mother's shoulder as if she were a newborn infant.

"Did you take your meds?" Farah asked.

"Yep! I'm ready to go."

"Well then….let's go find the place that's going to host the sweet sixteen party bash of all time."

****

They were already walking out of the front doors of the country club by the time Riley showed up to meet them. "Did I miss it?" she called out to the group from across the parking lot.

Callie moaned, "Here comes trouble."

"Be nice." Farah said between teeth that smiled at Riley from a distance.

Liv took a bedazzled flask from her purse and took a swig. "Here you want a hit to deal with her?" She asked Farah.

"Nope! Today is my day one." Farah said without emotion or making eye contact with anyone. She acted like it was no big deal that she decided to climb back on the wagon last night. But, the group knew what a major decision it was.

"That's great!" Callie said.

"Yeah, mom. That's awesome! I'm proud of you." Bryan gave her mother a high five.

By this time Riley and the group had met mid-way through the parking lot of the country club. Bryann gave Riley a very welcoming hug. "Thanks for coming to help."

"Sure thing." Riley said, "Anything for my little girl." It was a strain for her to sound maternal, but Riley knew the kinds of things she was supposed to say to a child she loved.

"Oh please," Callie said.

Liv offered Farah the flash one more time. "You sure?" When Farah ignored her she shrugged and turned it upside down in her mouth.

Riley looked at Liv. "Wow Olive. You drink about as much as I…"

"…Lie." Callie interrupted Riley's assumed criticism.

"No, I don't think she drinks that much," Riley said with a perfect smile.

It was that perfection that annoyed Callie and Riley knew it. She knew Callie hated her and she delighted in it. Ignoring Callie's sharp stare, Riley turned her attention to Farah. "Thanks again for inviting me to the Goodwyn's home. It was such a wonderful time. I even saw some people I know." She turned back to Callie with a pleasant grin – the kind you conjure when you are the only one in the room that knows a big secret.

"Really?" Liv slurred. "But you just got here."

"Yeah, well I make friends fast," Riley said. She winked at Callie who frowned back at her.

Farah tried to break the tension in the group. "Well, since Bryann has chosen this as her place, why don't we all grab a bite to eat?" Farah suggested.

"Oh, you decided already? But you finished so quickly." Riley said.

Callie sighed. "Actually we've been here for over an hour. We would have been finished a little sooner but we waited 20 minutes for you to show up."

Riley ignored her comments.

"I can't join you ladies for lunch. I have a date."

"Okay, no problem," Farah said. "Wait! A date? How do you have a lunch date if we were supposed to be out the whole day looking at venues for Bryann's party?"

"This is important so I was going to dip off and just catch back up to you guys later."

"Hmmm," Liv said. "A man more important than your daughter."

"What else is new?" Callie smirked.

"I'm actually having a quick lunch here…with my cousin Kane."

"Developing another devious plot to ruin families, huh?" Callie glared at Riley. She wanted so badly to slap Riley from the first day she saw her. The pain Riley had caused Farah angered Callie. Furthermore, Callie did not understand how Farah could be so nice to Riley.

Farah swallowed hard and she felt her cheeks heating up. If there was one thing her sobriety could not handle on DAY ONE it was Kane Taylor. Her heart filled with the heat of anger with slight chill of sadness.

"Don't mention his name to me." Farah said.

"Okay…fine, but…" Riley pointed her finger. All three of the girls turned back toward the building.

"Well I'll be damned," Liv hiccupped.

"You'll be drunk," Callie said. "Go sit in the car, Olive." She tossed the keys to Liv.

Liv tried to pick them up twice but stumbled each time, losing her balance. Bryann bent down and grabbed the keys for her. "I'll walk her to the car. C'mon Aunt Liv."

Farah turned around and watched Kane pull into a parking spot. She closed her eyes and said what she thought was equivalent to a prayer. Farah was never a religious person so she was not sure how to ask God for help but she needed it that very moment.

Farah smelled Kane as soon as his car door swung open. It was as if he moved in slow motion. In flat front pants and button down shirt, he looked like he had been given a fashion makeover. When he saw Farah, he smiled. She thought it stretched across his face as wide as land between oceans. And oceans were definitely flooding Farah at the moment. She never birthed at child but what she was feeling had to be analogous to having your water break.

"How can I still be so turned on by him?" she asked herself.

"Would you like to join us for lunch?" Riley asked.

"No." Callie responded because she saw the way Farah looked at Kane. It was clear that memories of their sex sessions in cars, parks, and balconies were running through her head.

"N..n..no," Farah managed to muster.

"You sure?" Riley said, "You look like you two need to talk. I'll tell you what. I'll take Bryann home in my car, Callie can drive Olive home and you and Kane have lunch and take all the time you need."

Farah just stood there in the parking lot staring at Kane. How they ended up in this space was well beyond her understanding as a woman and a psychiatrist. She had never allowed herself to love and then the first time she does, it turns out to be a sordid plan to destroy her family.

Farah frowned, "Nice try. You two set me up once. That was enough. I'm not sure what you thought was going to happen here today but whatever the plan was…you can cancel it."

"Yes, cancel it." Callie echoed.

Farah glared at her. Callie shined apologetic eyes.

Farah turned to Riley, "Let me be clear about something. I do not want to be anywhere near you. Either of you." She growled toward Kane. "But, I'm doing all of this because I love my daughter and I want her to have a healthy sense of family. The common bond among all of us is that we love Bryann. "

"Yes we do," Riley said.

"Then you better start acting like it," Farah said. "When I invite you to join us be on time. Don't make her an afterthought in your day. And don't you ever ever forget…I'm had my share of rough times too. You aren't the only one with a dysfunctional upbringing. You aren't the only one who knows how to scheme and manipulate the minds of other people to get what you want. I know it and I studied it in medical school. When it comes to game playing I'm like Parker Brother bitch. You got me?"

Kane took a step back. "Whoa Farah calm down. I'm sorry. I just wanted to see you."

"Shut up!" Farah never turned toward Kane but uttered her command strong and with conviction.

"The two of you better get your acts together quickly because Riley, I'm the only friend you have in this town."

"That's not exactly true," Riley said taking a step toward Farah. "And the next time you want to get courage…display it somewhere else.

Farah did not move. She raised her shoulders. The two women stood in the parking lot like lionesses preparing to battle of prey. Farah locked eyes with Riley, "You heard me."

"Yep, I did. But you got something wrong. I don't scheme or manipulate to get what I want. I command it." Riley swung around on her heels and strutted back to her car. She blew Bryann a kiss and pulled off.

Callie had gone back to the car, too. Now Farah and Kane just stood there in the parking lot. Her heart was filled with rage. She had some very familiar feelings rising up in side of her. She recalled the moments being in her room ripping sheets with her teeth because she had to display her anger in silence away from her Aunt Janice. All she wanted at the moment was a drink. Thank God Liv had certainly topped off the vodka in that flask.

"Just have dinner with me," Kane asked.

"No."

"Please."

"No."

"Okay, well just talk to me please."

"No," Farah said for the third time.

"Are you just going to stand there and say no?" Kane shook his head in defeat.

"Yes." She turned and walked away. After a few steps she called out to him. You know where to meet me. Tonight. 7pm. If you are 30 seconds late I am leaving."

"You won't regret it. I promise." Kane smiled.

-9-

Hidden Daylight was the perfect restaurant choice for Liv and Dylan to have a late afternoon dinner. The chef specialized in Italian cuisine and the owner specialized in keeping the confidence of his patrons. The quiet and dimly lit venue was a paradox. It was well known for being a secret place.

Everyone in the room assumed that the two people at the table next to them were lovers who had a reason to hide. The payment system helped to keep the identity of the patrons private. There was a flat price of admission to dine at the restaurant and everyone was assigned an alias, kind of like a username. So there were never any receipts to be found.

Hidden Daylight had been around for many years. Dylan and Liv heard about it from one of Dylan's brokers who not so innocently made a joke about taking him there. For two and a half years, Liv and Dylan met at the same table twice a week before heading off to their swanky 6-star suite at a nearby hotel.

"I have a 5:30 reservation for Peter and MJ." Dylan smiled at the hostess.

"Spiderman? Seriously?" Liv chuckled.

"I couldn't think of anything else at the time."

The hostess tossed her blonde hair back and smiled with deep silver blue eyes, "You aren't the only super hero here today." She laughed.

"Really?" Liv said in surprise.

"Of course not." The hostess grabbed two menus. "Follow me to your table."

Liv started by ordering a cosmopolitan. "…but with only a splash of cranberry please. I want it very light pink."

Dylan ordered a Macallan. Neat with rocks on the side.

Liv scanned all of the wedding bands and big diamond rings in the room. The people at the tables in Hidden Daylight were married… but not to each other.

"I want to start by saying I am sorry about the way things went last week." Dylan reached his hand across the table. "I was a little presumptuous of me but it was not meant to be offensive. I was just so excited to be with you again."

"You are not with me again," Liv asserted with her voice but extended her hand to be held across the table.

"Olive…we can pretend that this isn't happening but it is. We can pretend that we don't still love each other but we do."

"Dylan life is not about love. It's about commitment."

"Don't ridiculous, Olive. The only thing life is about is love."

Liv leaned back in her seat and looked at Dylan across the table. She was still very much in love with him but refused to start seeing him again. It took years for her to heal her heart and her marriage. This time she would be loyal. This time she was more focused on commitment than love.

Liv smiled at Dylan and crossed her arms. "Dylan, why was I waiting for you…. right down the street from here…with my bags packed full of all of my personal belongings?"

Dylan's face contorted but he remained silent.

"I believe that was eight years ago. Yes?" Liv paused for effect.

Dylan remained quiet and his normal shining eyes started to dim. He forced the corners of his mouth upward and began to look embarrassed. Nobody came to Hidden Daylight for this kind of conversation.

Liv nodded to answer her own question. "Yes. It was. My husband was at home in a panic-stricken fit. My mother-in-law came to the rescue and she still lives with me today because of it. By the way, thanks a lot for that one."

Liv returned Dylan's half grin. She could see the pain in his eyes. It matched the dull aching pain she felt in her chest. Every word brought her closer to tears but she refused to cry another tear for Dylan. She made herself that promise long ago.

Back then she waited days and weeks for Dylan to explain what happened. Weeks turned to months and those months turned into over a year. Finally, after 13 months, 2 weeks, and 4 days he called her to apologize for leaving her waiting in a hotel penthouse suite. At that time she was pregnant with her first child.

She locked eyes with him and continued. "Do you remember why all that happened? I'll tell you why. It wasn't love. It was commitment. You waited an entire year to call me," she whimpered. Finally, reluctant tears began to flow down her face. "…to call me and tell me that you were committed to taking care of Hannah. She was sick and you needed to stay with her. Commitment left me sitting in that hotel room with my bags ready to run away with you. Not love. Commitment… to your wife.

"At that moment, when we got off the telphone, I was determined to remain committed to my husband for he rest of our married lives. And I have done that. I will continue to do that. I am not interested in hearing you talk about love. I have made a commitment to my husband. I have a family now. Hell, I was so heartbroken over you I had four children back to back… to back… to back. Did you know that I have four sons?"

Dylan sat in silence and tears slowly streamed down Liv's buttermilk face at the thought of her children, who she believed, deserved a much better mother than her. The tip of her nose had turned red. The two sat in silence for what seemed like hours. Then the cocktails arrived.

Dylan smiled, this time showing his teeth. "All that before we even had a chance to make a toast." He chuckled deeply. "I love you Olive."

"I had never stepped outside of marriage before you or since you. Consider yourself the champion. It won't happen again."

"Then why did you come to the park to meet me?" he asked.

"To say the things I just said." She wiped her eyes. "But when you told me about Hannah I felt sorry for you. Then everything changed. But…I am back in my right mind and this…" Liv pointed back and forth across the table between the two of them. "…this is not going to happen."

Dylan looked up and over Liv's shoulder. "Oh no."

"What?" Liv turned around to see Farah and Kane being seated at the table behind them.

"Liv?" Farah whispered loudly when she saw her friend's face.

"MJ!" Liv whispered back quickly. Several tables shushed them and Liv frowned. "Ummm, my name is MJ."

Farah gathered herself and walked over to the table where Peter and MJ were sitting. Kane turned around in his chair.

"Oh shoot. I'm sorry. I'm Olivia." She looked at Kane. "That is Fitz."

Liv laughed through her stuffy nose and wiped beneath her eyes with her fingertips. "That's pretty good."

Kane waved his hand. "Thanks I came up with that one."

"So you guys come here?" Farah asked her friend.

"We used to..." Liv responded.

"Looks like you still do," Kane said.

"You...no talking," Farah said. "Just be glad you are back here again. Fitz!"

Kane laughed. "Alright then."

Dylan cleared his throat. "Are we not doing introductions?"

Liv and Farah looked at each other and frowned. Farah grimaced at Dylan. "Umm our husbands are best friends. I don't really need our boyfriends to be besties too. "

Liv jumped in. "No need for introductions. We were just leaving," Liv said. "And he's not my boyfriend. We just came here to set everything straight."

"We can't enjoy dinner together?" Dylan asked.

"Nope," Liv said. "And especially not now because I want no part of these two."

Kane looked surprised by Liv's comment. "Liv, I thought you were on our side. You believe I love Farah, don't you?"

"Not anymore Kane…uh.. Fitz. Besides, I used to think that Liv…Liv Pope, here…I used to think she should take you back but now I understand…." Liv paused and her lip began to quiver. She looked at Dylan. "Now I understand that what's done is done."

Liv quickly gulped her light pink cosmo, grabbed her bag and walked away from the table. Dylan jumped up to chase behind her. "Olive!"

Farah grabbed his arm. "Dylan, I'm going to tell you this as a professional psychiatrist and as Liv's friend. Let her go. She honored your choice. Now you honor hers."

Dylan opened his mouth to speak but he thought about what Farah said. She was right. "You know, Olive never once questioned my decision to stay with Hannah. She did not pressure me that day or any day since then. You are so right." He sat back down at the table. "Do you two mind if I sit here for just a few minutes to finish my drink? I need to clear my head."

"No problem, man," Kane said and Farah frowned. "Oh sorry. I guess I still can't speak."

"No you can't." Farah turned away from Kane back to Dylan. "Finish your drink. Give her time to leave."

Dylan's eyes widened. "Oh shoot, we drove together."

Farah flashed her phone to Dylan and showed him Liv's text message. It read, "Thank God for Uber."

They both laughed and Farah moved back to her table with "Fitz" who had already ordered drinks and appetizers for both of them.

– 10 –

The fire between Farah and Kane had definitely fizzled. Farah was methodical, concise, and unemotional in her speech. Kane was compassionate, apologetic and right down sad in his plea for Farah's forgiveness.

"I never intended to hurt you," he said.

"You are certainly delusional. That is precisely what you intended to do. That's why your cousin hired you." Farah responded with hollow eyes and an empty heart.

"Yes, you're right. I allowed Riley to manipulate me into doing her dirty work. I was wrong. I had no idea that we would fall in love." Kane dipped his head and then looked back up at Farah. "I love you, Farah."

"Love is honest. Love is kind. Love is a bunch of stuff in the Bible. I've never read it but I've heard it enough."

Kane looked at Farah. Suddenly his eyes got brighter his face was no longer sagging and sullen.

"What?" Farah asked. "There's a light bulb over your head. What are you thinking?"

"Farah, let's pray."

Farah roared with laughter. "Pray? To who?"

"To God." Kane said and pointed upward. "You don't believe me. You don't think I love you. Ask God and he will tell you."

"I don't know God. We've never met." She jeered.

"Well let me introduce you. Would you go to church with me on Sunday?"

"No!" Farah puckered her face like she had eaten a whole lemon…peeling and all. "You cannot be serious right now. Kane, my life is in a complete shambles because of you and your cousin. Everything I thought I knew about you was wrong. The person I fell in love with was not you. It was someone else. A false representative of a man."

"No, that's not true. I am exactly who you know. The man doing Riley's bidding, that was a false man." Kane begged.

"Kane, I don't know how to fix this." Farah said. She shook her head. "Too much has happened. It's too late."

"God can fix it. It's never too late." Kane said.

"Where is all this God coming from? Since when did you become a God person?"

"I've always been a God person…"

Farah raised her eyebrows. "Really?"

"Yes. Okay, I may not have been the best God person but I have always believed in God and I know he has watched over me my entire life."

Farah listened, but did not respond.

"I started going to church after that day in court. I asked God for forgiveness for all that I had done. I even prayed for you, Greg, and Bryann to make it through."

Farah sat still. Kane knew she was listening, but neither her face nor her body showed any signs.

"Farah I love you enough to let you go. I do. If you tell me right now that you love Greg and you want to be married to him because you love him then I will walk out of this place and never bother you again."

Farah opened her mouth to speak…but Kane interrupted her.

"Before you spout out something you don't mean. At least take time to think about what I'm saying."

Farah thought for a moment. There was no amount of time that would change her mind, but to keep from making a scene and to enjoy the delightful manicotti in front of her she agreed.

The two sat and ate their dinner together trying to stay away from any topics that would cause debate or resurface their issues. They talked about current events and Kane told Farah about the latest psychology books he had been reading.

"I learned a lot about myself during this time."

Farah took one last bite from her plate and leaned back. She was engaged in what Kane was saying but she was also full to her eyes with pasta. "Tell me what you learned."

Kane took a deep breath. "I learned that I've always felt like I wasn't good enough. After I lost my scholarship and came home to work this job…I felt like a complete failure. I should have a PhD by now."

"Slow down…" Farah joked.

Kane laughed. "Okay at least my masters in psychology."

Farah thought back to the very first time she and Kane met for coffee. He shared so many surprising things with her. He was very well rounded with a lot of different interests. He loved everything from dominos to deep sea diving. He was very well read, especially in the area of psychology and self-help techniques. Kane wanted to be a psychologist, but after his NCAA violation the only thing left for him was driving a truck for the package delivery company. A good job.

"Kane, you can still go back to school."

"It's too late," Kane said.

"Did you just tell me it's never too late?" Farah smiled at him.

Kane bellowed a small chuckle. "Yes I did."

"Then maybe you should pray about it," Farah mocked.

"Maybe I will," Kane asserted. "Can I pray for you?"

"What? No. Here? No."

"Give me your hand…"

Farah reluctantly stretched her arms across the table and bowed her head. She felt the room staring at them.

Kane began to pray. "Father God, please forgive us of our sins. We know that the way we live is not pleasing to you. So much has happened between Farah and me and we need your help. We need your clarity. We need your wisdom. Lord I ask that you touch Farah's heart to let her know the plan you have for her and her family. I also ask that you show her the plan that you have for us together. Let our love be pleasing to you. Let it not be rooted in lust or selfish gain but in your love because you are love God. In Jesus name we pray this prayer fully expecting an answer. Amen"

When Kane and Farah raised their heads the owner was standing at their table. He bent down and whispered something to Kane. Kane nodded and the owner walked away.

"Umm, we gotta go." He said.

"Why? I want dessert." Farah asserted.

"Well, I guess you could say we are being kicked out."

Farah looked around the restaurant and several tables were frowning at them. One man looked as if he wanted to come over and choke Kane. The woman at his table was now crying and shaking her head.

Farah and Kane got up from their table and slowly walked to the door with the entire restaurant watching them. Some were frowning with a look of "good riddance" on their faces. Others looked like they wanted to get up and walk out behind them.

When they got outside, Kane reached over to grab Farah's hands again. "Just pray about it," he said.

Farah pouted a bit, "But I don't know how to pray. I could not do what you just did. You shut down the creep spot. Look…" She pointed toward the door where two separate couples were leaving. The looks on their faces told it all.

"Praying is just talking to God."

"Okay, but you are not making any sense. So, you want me to pray and ask God if I can have an affair with you? That doesn't seem right to me and I've never been to Sunday school in my life."

"No Farah. I want you to pray about being my wife."

Farah stood in astonishment for a moment. She sighed. "That was our plan wasn't it?"

"Yes, it was." Kane said. "And it can still be God's plan for us."

"I don't know." Farah looked off in the distance. "I just don't know what to do."

-11-

Over a month had gone by and Farah had not spoken to Kane or seen Liv face to face. It was as if everyone wanted to erase that day in Hidden Daylight as if it never happened. But it did happen and it had Farah confounded. She had not prayed yet. She was busy trying to reinstate her sobriety and plan Bryann's party.

But lately she was bothered by the talk she had with Kane. She thought of it every night before she fell off to sleep alone in her room. Finally she decided to talk to her best friend about it.

"So he told me to pray." Farah told Callie.

"Pray? To who?"

"THAT'S WHAT I SAID!" Farah squealed. She and her best friend were cut from the same cloth. "To God," Farah said with expectation of Callie's response.

"Oh honey, God is not checking for girls like us. You know this."

Farah nodded in agreement. "Yeah, but what if he is?"

"He's not!" Callie asserted. "Really? So this God took my birth parents away, my fiancé away, my adoptive parents away and one of my brothers. He clearly wants me to know that I am alone."

Callie made a strong point. Since they were young girls, the two of them understood that they were on their own in this world. Farah's Aunt Janice was bitter about having to care for her. She reminded Farah what a burden she was every day of her life. Though Callie had wonderful adoptive parents and siblings, she never allowed herself to be comfortable. She always knew deep down inside that they would go away.

Callie continued, "When my mom got sick I was devastated."

"I remember."

"So God had given me this great family and then gives my mom cancer? Really?" Callie shook her head. "When mom died I knew Dad would not last long after her. Every day I prayed to God to keep my dad safe. When the hospital called me I knew he was going to die. His heart stopped before I could even get to him. My dad died of a broken heart."

Farah listened. Her eyes had begun to tear. She had lived this once with her friend, Callie. They were only nineteen at the time. Now it was if she was living it again.

"But that wasn't enough loss for me. No, oh no…God was afraid I wouldn't get it. So I buried my mother. Then three months later I buried my father and the same day my brother takes his life?"

Callie did not have even a slight mist in her eyes. Her shoulders were thrown back and her face was like stone. "I buried them all. The only family I ever knew. And God, as you say, took them all away from me….and don't say I still have Robbie because we know he has not been worth the price of a wet paper bag since Matt died."

Farah nodded. Callie was telling the truth. Her other brother Matt never recovered from the death of his family. He isolated himself from everyone, even his sister.

"So Farah, I can appreciate the fact that you want to wrap all of this mess up in a nice, neat little bow. And you think that talking to the clouds is going to help you do that. But sometimes things are meant to be broken."

At that point, Farah had no words for her friend. Four years of psychology, four years of medical school, four years of residency and three years of specialty fellowship did not give Farah any response to her friend's perspective. Farah had fixed a lot of messes in her time as a psychiatrist, but Callie was right…this fractured bunch was going to take some serious psychological super glue to keep together.

"You know, maybe we ought to just try to pray and see what happens."

"Well you go ahead and knock yourself out on that one. Pray about not knowing who your dad is or what your true ethnicity is. Pray about your mom being dead. Pray about being an alcoholic with a bipolar daughter. Pray about that evil witch Riley, who lives to destroy your family. Pray about all of that and let me know what you come up with. Oh…and don't forget to pray for God to reunite you with the husband you never loved so you can continue to be in the streets with men, miserable but still in the same house as a family."

Perplexed at her friend's anger, Farah looked at Callie. "Ouch!"

"I'm sorry."

"No you are not. You said what you meant."

"No I didn't mean that Farah. You know I didn't."

"YES, you did." Farah concluded. "My schooling and practice may not allow me to solve this huge problem in my life but there are some things I know without a doubt. People never say things they don't mean. They sometimes say things that they never meant to say."

Callie and Farah hugged at the door and Callie apologized again before she left the house. She started to walk down the sidewalk and turned back to Farah.

"What's up with girlfriend?" Callie asked. She pointed over to Adam and Liv's house.

"I'm not completely sure. I talked to her yesterday but I still haven't seen her."

"Where is she? Just sitting in the house?"

"No, she's been doing some things with the boys' school and I think she rejoined her sorority."

"Really?" Callie scrunched her nose.

"Yep. You should call her."

"I might call her when I get home." Callie blew a kiss to Farah and jumped in her car.

-12-

Maybe Callie was right. Maybe God picked some people to be broken. But why did he choose her to be one of them? She had suffered so much loss in her life. It seemed unrealistic for there to be some kind of God out there that loved her.

Farah believed in God. She was simply unsure of what his deal was. She wanted to pray but she did not know where to start. Kane told her to just talk to God. She had tried that a couple of times but it felt silly. So she sat in silence for a while.

Finally she picked up her phone. "Can you come over?" She asked the voice on the other end of the line. "I'm lonely and I think I want to pray."

Farah continued to sit on the sofa. She replayed the events of the last year over in her head. It was almost a year ago that she sat in that very room and took a drink breaking over ten years of sobriety.

She looked around the room and envisioned the way Greg had thrown the photographs all over the floor. Every place she looked she saw still shots of her having sex with Kane…in the back seat of a black sedan. She remembered when Greg saw the shot of the two of them coming out of the New York apartment.

Farah cringed at the memory. She had purchased an apartment for Kane so they could be together in private. Ironically that was the day Riley hired the photographer to follow them.

Farah wondered how God could have allowed that to happen to her. If God did not like what she was doing, why didn't he stop her from marrying Greg all those years ago? Why would God allow her to marry someone only to destroy the family sixteen years later? Farah concluded that Callie was right. Some things are just meant to be broken.

She collapsed herself over on the arm of the sofa and sighed. "Why can't psychiatry make me feel better right now?"

Just then the doorbell rang but Farah didn't move. It rang again. She sat up, but didn't go to the door. A few seconds later Greg walked in. "Why didn't you get the door?"

Farah looked up at him, "You have a key."

Greg sat down in the chair across from her. "So what's going on? You said you want to pray. Am I missing something?"

"No. I don't know. Maybe." Farah bumbled her words. "I think I want to pray."

"Where is this coming from?" Greg asked.

Farah thought for a moment. She knew if she told Greg that Kane suggested she pray that Greg would walk right out the door. So she decided not to tell him exactly where she got the suggestion.

"I feel like we've tried everything else. We need to pray."

Greg, whose most powerful entity was money, gave his estranged wife a crooked look. "This is a little strange, Farah."

"I know. It's different but maybe we need something different." She said.

There was a buzz from his pocket and Greg looked down at his phone. He silenced the buzz and kept talking. "Well, do you know how to pray? I don't know how to pray. I could call my mother."

"Oh please! I'm sure the God that your mom and her friends worship on Sunday only likes whites – like them." Farah rolled her eyes. "Okay that was mean but seriously. The last thing we need is your mother involved."

"I agree with you on that." Greg's phone buzzed again. This time it was a text message. He looked at it and smiled.

"Oh wow! I haven't seen a smile like that in a long time."

"What smile?" Greg asked.

"The one you just wiped off of your face," Farah charged. "So you met someone?"

"No I didn't meet someone."

"So you already knew her but something different is going on between you now." Farah said. She was the master of dating affairs. She knew exactly the way that smitten and predatory women sit back and wait on tragedy to strike the relationship of someone they are interested in pursuing. She had done it many times. "Jessica?"

"How did you know that?" Greg asked. His voice was confounded in tone.

"Well, let's see…" Farah started, "She is over complimentary of you. She always asks you for help on things that require little or no skill…"

"That's not true," Greg interrupted.

"It is too," Farah charged. She mocked in a high voice. "Greg can you tell me how to work the pencil sharpener. Do you turn the pencil to the left or to the right?"

Greg laughed. "You are something else, Dr. Goodwyn."

"Thank you Mr. Goodwyn. I am good at what I do."

Greg sighed. "Yes it's Jessica. We've been out a few times."

The smile on Greg's face made Farah uncomfortable. He did not realize that he was smiling at the thought of his time with Jessica.

Farah leaned in to him. "You're smitten."

"Maybe a little," he said.

"No maybe. You are."

Greg took a deep breath. "Farah do you love Kane?"

"No! I told you that." Farah asserted and slid down the sofa to be closer to where Greg sat. "I was caught up in emotion. I wanted something to make me feel better. I realize I have a lot of issues when it comes to intimacy and my desire to feel good."

Greg nodded, "Okay let me ask you another question…do you love me?"

Farah grinned. Care and concern filled her eyes. Warmth and respect filled her heart. She looked at Greg and spoke in complete honesty. "I don't think so."

"Did you ever love me?'

"I don't think so." Farah said.

For Farah, the moment she told Greg that she didn't love him, was actually the moment she realized that she did. But she loved him in a different way than what he needed to be loved. She loved him as a brother, a good friend. She did not love him as a mate or a partner. From the beginning she had only seen him as a means to a life that she wanted to create. She had grown to love Greg greatly, but in her mind that was not the kind of love a marriage required. She wanted passionate love, deep love, and penetrating love.

Farah went over and sat on Greg's lap the way she had done since college. She was his little piece of chocolate heaven and he was her white knight in shining armor.

She kissed him on the cheek. "You know, they say that prayer is just talking to God. Maybe we should try it. I've never prayed before to anyone but my mother. And I stopped doing that a while ago."

"Well, it's worth a shot." Greg said. "Let's do it!"

"Okay, what do we do?" Farah asked.

"I guess we just start talking."

The two looked at each other. A weight was lifted from Farah's shoulders. The pressure to win Greg back had left her. She wasn't sure how she would tell Bryann but she was certain that her marriage was over.

She bowed her head and closed her eyes. Greg grabbed her hands. Farah started to pray. "God…I don't really know how to do this, but I guess I just talk to you. I've tried this before but I don't think you hear me. If you know my mother she can tell you about me. I know she must be up there with you."

Greg remained quiet.

Farah continued. "We made a mess of this marriage God. I'm so sorry I have hurt the people I love…"

Greg interjected, "…and I am so sorry I have ignored the people I love."

Farah opened one eye and saw that Greg's head was bowed with his eyes closed too. Farah continued, "Help us to fix this for our daughter. Help us to love her even if we are apart."

Greg cut in again, "And God, please give Farah time to heal and to be the wonderful, smart, beautiful woman she is. I hope she learns who she is. While she takes care of her patients, please let her take care of herself too."

"And God help Greg to be smart and funny and kind and successful. Maybe he can find a wife that deserves to be with someone so great."

Then they were both quiet. They peeked at each other. "Is this where we say Amen?" Farah asked.

"I think so. If we are finished talking."

"Okay Amen God."

"Amen," Greg said.

Farah exhaled. "That wasn't so bad I guess. Now what?"

"I don't know. I think that's it."

Greg stood up and lifted his wife. He cradled her in his arms the way he did when he carried her through the doors of the house. They locked eyes. Farah saw twenty-five years of life in Greg's eyes. From their college days, to bringing home their daughter, to pulling into his parents driveway back in April they had built a life of memories that would last forever.

"Oh okay. So what do we do now?" Farah asked.

Greg's jaw became strong and he said sweetly, "I guess we file paperwork."

He lowered her to the floor and they embraced in what seemed like a final embrace. They would spend many more years together sharing special moments, graduations, weddings, and holidays as co-parents and grandparents. But this would be the last time they embraced as husband and wife.

Greg cleared his throat. "I have to tell you something."

Farah broke the embrace and looked up at him. She braced herself for the worst. Was Jessica pregnant? Was he getting married? Was he moving her in with him? Farah's heart started to beat faster. She swallowed and gathered her composure.

"Yes?" She said calmly.

"You know Acer and Callie are sleeping together, right?"

"Yes, I know that. I'm trying not to get excited about the possibilities." Farah said.

"Good." Greg paused. "Because he was sleeping with Riley too."

"WHAT!!!!!!" Farah fell back on the sofa. "Are you kidding me?"

"I wish I was," Greg said. "When she showed up at Mom and Dad's anniversary party he freaked. He had no idea she was Bryann's birthmother and that she would ever be anywhere near the family."

"What the…? Huh? Wait…how did they meet?" Farah asked.

"I'm not sure but he hasn't seen her since that day at our parent's house. But, he's afraid Callie is going to find out and then…"

"Oh God! Talk about prayer…"

"Exactly," Greg said.

"So what do we do?" Farah asked.

"Well, he wants you to tell her." Greg said with a sheepish grin.

"Me? Why me?"

"Because you can do it in a way that keeps her calm. Use some psycho tools and hypnosis or something."

"Oh God!" Farah thought for a minute. "I've spent my whole life not talking to God. Now I feel like I need to do a marathon session with him."

-13-

Several weeks had passed since Greg dropped the news on Farah. She had seen Callie a number of times but never felt like it was the right time to tell her.

Acer came into the kitchen and startled Farah. "Did you tell her yet?" He whispered to his soon-to-be ex-sister-in-law.

"No, and I don't see why I have to be the one to tell her," Farah whispered back. "Besides if I had told her you would certainly know by the swelling in your eye." She laughed.

"Not funny." Acer said.

The two of them hovered in the corner of the kitchen. The rest of the gang was in the dining room waiting for dessert to be served. Farah and Greg had invited Adam and Liv, Callie and Acer over to the house to announce their decision to divorce. It came as a shock to everyone. Not the divorce, but the fact that they had planned such an elaborate and loving dinner together to tell their friends.

Callie burst through the kitchen doors. "What's taking you two so long? Where's the cake?"

"You know," Farah said. She put her hand on her rounded hips, "It gets on my nerves that you eat as much cake as you do and never gain a single pound."

Callie shrugged. "Well, hey! That's something Riley and I have in common. Maybe we can bond over that."

Farah and Acer looked at one another. When Callie spun around on her heels and sashayed back into the dining room Farah said under her breath, "That's not all you two have in common."

Acer frowned, "C'mon sis. Please help me. I love Callie. You know I do."

Farah sighed. "Yes, I know you do." She shook her head. "You better not mess this up again."

He grabbed her around her shoulders and gave her a huge baby brother hug. "Thank you! You may be getting a divorce but you will always be my sister. I love you and my niece."

"I know. I know. Get out of here and let me bring in the cake. Here, take these." She handed Acer the plates and dessert forks.

Farah brought the cake in the family room, "Let's all come in here by the fireplace."

She flipped the switch and fire rose from beneath the ceramic logs. The others filed into the room. They were laughing and chatting like old times. Liv seemed to have recovered from her "moment" with Dylan and things were back to normal. Callie and Acer had progressed. They were at least admitting that they cared for each other, which was a huge deal for those two stone hearts.

Greg and Farah had moved swiftly through mediation over the past couple of months and their divorce would be final in 30 days. Things were going well and she did not want to disrupt the flow of normalcy with the news of Riley and Acer.

She had an idea. She called Greg into the kitchen.

"What's up?" he asked.

"I have an idea."

"Uh oh!" he said.

"No seriously, I have an idea that could work very well for everyone." Farah was nodding her head in affirmation of her thought.

"Go on." Greg said, "I'm listening."

"Instead of telling Callie about Acer, why don't I just go to talk to Riley. She's changed so much. I'll just go talk to her and let her know that she needs to keep that quiet."

"Let me make sure I understand this. You want to appeal to the kindness inside of the woman who devised a year long plan to wreck our family?"

"Yes," Farah said with bright eyes.

"And you think she will care enough about Callie's happiness with Acer that she'll keep their affair quiet?"

"Yes!" Farah nodded again this time her eyes were even brighter. She believed in her idea so much that she completely missed Greg's sarcasm.

"Sounds good." He shrugged and turned as if to walk away. Then he turned around. "Oh and while you're at it can you see if my mom wants to join the NAACP?"

Farah gasped and folded her arms. "Greg! I'm serious."

"I know you are and that is exactly what scares me. Farah, that woman cares for no one but herself. I'm not so sure she cares for herself. She doesn't care for Bryann. She doesn't care for you and she most certainly doesn't care for Callie."

"It's worth a shot," Farah said. "If it doesn't work then I'll tell Callie."

Farah and Greg went back into the family room. The other couples were appropriately cuddled up on the two love seats. Callie and Acer pawed all over each other. It wasn't the newness of the relationship because they had been on and off since Farah and Greg married. The two of them were just hot for each other, pure and simple. They were the perfect matches for one another. Despite how dysfunctional they were individually, they actually worked as a couple.

Adam and Liv looked like newlyweds again. Liv actually looked happy not just because she had four drinks at dinner. Farah was pleased to hear that Liv was not drinking everyday anymore. She had reengaged with the boys and Adam. She seemed to have accepted her fate as a mother and housewife – with a Georgetown law degree.

"Well, since we are sharing news I guess I'll share mine." Adam stood to his feet. "I have made a decision to sell my practice into a system."

Liv looked up at her husband like it was the first time she was hearing this too. Farah was concerned about the look on Liv's face. Callie made eye contact with Farah. It was clear this was a surprise to Liv. Adam had not made this little announcement to his wife yet.

Adam continued, "I was approached by a very successful company that helps solo private practice guys like me prepare for the future. Liv and I are doing so well. The boys are happy and healthy. I want to spend more time with my family."

Liv spoke with a frog in her throat. "What's the name of the company?"

"Future Health Connect."

Callie and Farah looked at each other. Their eyes were wide as teacups. Farah tried not to show any change in body language. She was so good at this with her patients but when it came to her personal friends and family, it was as if she never spent a day in medical school.

Greg chimed in, "That's great!"

Acer echoed, "Yeah, man. Congratulations. I'm sure there is a nice pay check that comes with that."

"It's alright." Adam grinned. "I'll be making that Greg Goodwyn money now." He and Acer slapped five. "Especially since he's giving half to Farah."

They all laughed.

"Not half," Farah said.

"Just about half," Greg said. "But gladly. Farah was and still is the love of my life. She's the mother of my daughter and I want nothing but happiness for her."

"Aww thanks, sweetheart." Farah stood to her feet.

Liv was very quiet. Callie and Farah tried to push past the moment but they didn't get there fast enough before Liv spoke. "So Adam." She paused and squinted at him. "When were you going to discuss this with me?"

"It all happened so fast, darling. I was going to wait to tell you but this seemed like the right time since everyone else was sharing happy news."

"Happy news? Farah and Greg are divorcing. That's not happy news."

"You know what I mean."

"No I don't know what you mean, Adam."

"Olive…"

"Don't call me that," Liv asserted. She held her stomach as if she were nauseous at the sound of Adam's voice.

"But that's your name."

"Please, don't call me that."

"Okay…okay… Liv." Adam said, "I'm doing this for us. I'm doing this for our family."

Farah wanted to call a time out but Greg held his hand up to hold her back in her seat. There was something about that darn family room that got couples in trouble. Farah made a mental note to completely redecorate the room. It needed to be something else because "family" did not have a good run in that room.

Liv sat back and started eating her cake. Farah was happy to see her eat cake rather than pulling a flask from her bag. She ate the cake and asked for another glass of wine. When Farah got up to go the kitchen, Liv followed. "I'll come with you."

She tapped Callie's knee while making her way to the kitchen. Acer nodded for Callie to go to the group meeting about to happen in the kitchen.

As soon as the three of them got far enough away from the men, Callie and Farah asked at the exact same time. "Is that Dylan's company?"

"YES!" Liv said in a strong tenor voice that made Callie wince.

"I was afraid of that." Farah said.

"I know Dylan is doing this on purpose. I know it." Liv said.

"Well, why would he be trying to free up Adam's time for you two to be together more? That is not a great strategy to break up your marriage."

"Hmmm, I don't know but I know he's up to something."

"Well you cannot let Adam know it's Dylan's company," Callie said.

"Why not?" Liv asked.

Callie growled, "Oh, good thing I'm a detective or else you two would always end up in trouble."

Farah interrupted, "Yeah because you have done such a great job keeping us out of trouble so far."

"Whatever," Callie scoffed and turned her attention back to Liv. "Because when you were with Dylan he was a venture capitalist. How will you explain that you know he owns this company?"

"Ohhhh" Farah nodded, "Good point."

"Shoot!" Liv agreed with Callie's point. "Well we have to do something because when Adam finds out Dylan is behind this. Oh Dear Lord."

"You two and your prayers..." Callie said.

"Hey! It works," Farah said. "I've even started to incorporate it into my treatment plans for patients. They all come back and say it works."

"It's all in your head. You do know that right?" Callie asked.

"Maybe." Farah said, "But things are getting back to normal and I think it's because I pray.

"Okay," Callie said. "Well keep on praying because this is going to be explosive."

"It's not the only thing," Farah said under her breath.

"What?" Callie asked. "I didn't hear you."

"Nothing." Farah smiled. "Everything will be fine."

- 14 -

Farah sat in the back of the coffee shop with her iPad. For a chilly Saturday morning the shop was surprisingly empty. There were fewer than twenty people, which was quite unusual.

When Kane walked in the shop he was smiling from ear to ear. He had a fresh haircut and his face was clean-shaven. Farah thought of how different he looked from the first time they had met in this shop a year ago. Kane said he was different. Whether or not that was true, he certainly looked different.

"Good morning!" Kane cheered.

"Hey you." Farah said with a smile.

"Should I sit at the table next to you?" Kane mocked.

The first time they met at this coffee shop Farah would not allow Kane to sit at the same table with her. She said they could have coffee in the same place at the same time, but not "together". So they sat at separate tables and talked for sometime before eventually joining each other. That was the beginning of their affair.

"Stop it. Sit down." Farah laughed.

Kane sat across from her at the table. When he removed his scarf and coat, she noticed he had a small cross around his neck. Kane looked different. He was still very strong and handsome looking but there was something softer about him. Something peaceful.

"You look great!" Farah said with enthusiasm. "Wow!"

"Thanks! I feel great."

She reached across the table and grabbed his bicep and Kane grunted.

"Ouch!"

Farah jumped back, "What? What happened?"

"Kane rolled up his shirt sleeve. I got a new tattoo and you just squeezed it like an orange. Ouch!"

"Oh I'm sorry, let me see it." Farah said.

Kane turned his body to the side with his arm facing Farah. He had a fresh tattoo. His arm was still red and swollen. The ink was puffy but Farah could still get a good look at it. It was a cross like the one around his neck. It read "JESUS" in an arch above the cross. Beneath the cross there was a scripture. It said "2 Corinthians 5:17."

"What does that mean?" Farah asked pointing at the scripture.

"It's the scripture for my life. It says, 'Therefore, if anyone is in Christ, he is a new creation; old things have passed away; behold all things have become new. "

"Wow! That's really cool, Kane."

"Yeah, it is. I feel like a new person so when people tell me I look different I just thank God. I'm not the same person Farah."

"I can see that." She smiled then hung her head a bit. "I wish I could do that. You just wiped away your old self. That's amazing. I talk to my clients all the time about recreating themselves after unpleasant situations in life. You are the first person I see who had actually done that. Wow!"

"It wasn't me that did it Farah. It was God."

Farah's face went blank. "Yeah, I've been talking to him a little bit. But, he's not making me new like you."

"Did you ask him?" Kane's inquiry made Farah think for a moment.

"Kane, I didn't come here to talk about God."

Kane threw both palms up in front of him. "Okay. Okay."

"Thanks," Farah dismissed. "So, Greg and I are divorcing. It is very amicable and I think we are in a really good place."

"I'm sorry to hear that Farah."

"You are?"

"Of course I am." He said. "I know how painful this is for all of you. Even if I think it's the right decision for you I know it's hard."

Farah looked at Kane with a puzzled look. "Who are you?"

Kane laughed. "I'm a new creation. But one thing is the same."

"What's that?" Farah asked.

"I still love you. I'm so sorry for everything I did to cause you pain."

"So you think because you have a cross on your arm and around your neck everything is all better and we are supposed to run off in love? C'mon Kane. You should know me better than that."

"I do." He said. "But I also know that you can change. God can change you."

"Honey, if God were going to change me he would have done that by now."

"Did you ask him? God doesn't go around with a magic wand zapping people into a new life."

"Anyway," Farah changed the subject once again. "My life is moving forward and I just want to let you know."

"Thank you." He said.

"Why haven't you called me?"

"I wanted you to have some space to think. But I prayed for you every day."

"I needed two months?"

"It guess so," he said.

"That's a lot different from the guy who called me twenty times in a day, every day for weeks."

"Because it's not the same guy."

"I see that."

"Look Farah. I love you. But I love God enough to trust that whatever he wants this relationship to be it will be."

Farah listened to him.

Kane continued, "I believe God can fix this situation. We started out as a mess…like David and Bathsheba…but God brought Jesus through that."

"Okay, I don't know David or that other person you said. I don't know a lot about religion but I know that what we did was wrong. You don't need to be a Bible scholar to know that."

"Yes it was but…" Kane turned and pointed to the scripture beneath his tattoo.

Farah nodded. She could see that Kane was pretty serious about this new life of his. It was kind of cute and refreshing. "You want to go to dinner tonight?" she asked.

Kane smile. "No."

"No?" Farah gasped. She was truly shocked.

"Farah, I don't want an affair with you. I don't want secret dinners and sex. I want a true relationship. I want you to be my wife."

"That's probably not going to happen," Farah asserted.

"So be it," Kane said. "I will continue to pray."

"Yep, you do that." Farah leaned in to Kane. "You know, some things are meant to be broken."

"That sounds like something Callista would say."

Farah frowned. "Yes, Callie said it but I agree with her. I believed it."

Kane thought for a moment. "Humph. Then why be a psychiatrist?"

"What are you talking about?"

"If you believe some things are made to be broken, then why be a psychiatrist?"

Farah gave that some thought. He made a good point. As a psychiatrist, she believed that everyone and everything could be fixed by either intensive therapy or medication. Most of the time, it required both. Kane got her on that one but she refuse to surrender to his comment.

"Well, hey, it was good catching up with you. I'm glad you are doing well. If you ever want to grab dinner or something let me know. If I never see you again…I'll understand." She got up from the table and grabbed her things. "So I better get going."

Kane stood to his feet. He kissed her on the cheek in a very friendly way. "Take Care beautiful. I'll be praying for you."

-15-

The party came upon them quickly. Bryann was excited as Farah had ever seen her. "Oh thank you, Mom! My sweet sixteen is going to be the best one in the whole school."

Farah hugged her daughter. "You're welcome. We love you."

Bryann thought for a moment. "Mom?"

"Yes honey." Farah continued to put on her lipstick. They both looked at each other through the mirror instead of turning toward one another.

"Are you going to be okay with Dad's girlfriend coming to my party?"

Farah swallowed. She had not realized that the divorce and new life was still weighing on her daughter. Even after all of these months Bryann had not gotten used to her parents being apart. She was not always pleasant toward Jessica, Greg's girlfriend.

Farah smiled a huge smile showing her teeth and her eyes shined with happiness. "Of course. I am very happy for Dad. But I am not a big Jessica fan. I'll admit. But I'm happy that Dad is happy. Besides, this party is about you, not me, not Dad, and certainly not Jessica."

"It's not about Riley either." Bryann said.

"Nope."

"But when she's sees Kendall coming into that party she is going to flip out." Bryann laughed at the thought. "It's going to be interesting."

"I don't think she'll do that. She's come a long way in this past year, honey. Riley has been pretty quiet."

"Did she ever tell Aunt Callie about Uncle Acer?"

"No, she didn't. After the talk I had with her we agreed that being apart of this family would require her to love and care for everyone. Sometimes you have to put your own desires aside."

"I still can't believe she went for that. She is clearly the most selfish person I have ever met. I have two moms. One who is the most selfless person in the world and the other the most selfish. Yes, I am bipolar."

"Bryann!!!" Farah laughed. They both laughed together. "Speaking of… did you take your medicine?"

"Yep. I have not missed a dose in almost six months. I don't want anything to ruin this party." Bryann said proudly.

"Me either." Farah gave her daughter a high five. "You ready? Let's go." They walked downstairs and got into the bubblegum pink stretch hummer, just the two of them. They shared some girl talk on the way over and Farah continued to tell Bryann how proud she was to be chosen as her mother.

Bryann had been apart of all of the planning so it was hard for Farah to find an element of surprise, but she had found one. Bryann thought that her party started at 9pm and they were going early. In fact Farah had told all the guests to arrive by 7pm so they could be there to receive the birthday girl. Though Bryann had seen (and had to approve) most of the decorations, Farah added a few elements for her daughter.

"A red carpet!!!" Bryann screamed when they pulled into the lot.

Everyone was outside lined on both sides of the carpet. There were signs and cameras. Bryann had her own paparazzi. When she got out of the Limo, everyone began to shout her name. The seven photographers called out to her with every step she took. "Bryann. Bryann. Look this way."

"Oh my goodness Mom! This is awesome!!"

Greg stood at the top of the red carpet, ready to receive his daughter. Farah walked her half way down the red carpet and then she let her daughter walk the rest of the way to be greeted by her father. Farah stood on the carpet and it was like there was no one else around. She had a private thought, lost in a moment of peace. It had all come together so nicely.

The crowd moved inside and the party began. The DJ played great music for the kids. The food was phenomenal and Bryann was the happiest Farah had seen her since the day she learned to roller skate when she was seven years old. Surprisingly, Farah and Jessica were getting along nicely.

Callie pulled Farah off into the corner, "Hey! Not that I care but where are those other people?"

"Who?" Farah asked.

"Riley and the birth father. What's his name? Kendall."

"Oh shoot!"

In all the excitement Farah did not realize that Riley had not shown up yet. She started to panic and wonder if she had told Riley to arrive at 7pm, but she was sure she did.

"Well, Kendall and his wife were delayed coming out of Michigan, but they have arrived and are in the car on their way here now." Farah explained.

Liv bopped her way across the dance floor over to the girls. "Hey Ladies!" She sang. "Is everything okay over here?"

"Yeah, it's fine." Farah said. "We just realized that Riley is missing."

Liv looked around the room. "Oh yeah." She shrugged. "Well good."

"Liv!" Farah scolded. "She's Bryann's birthmother. You guys are going to have to get used to her. Geez, you two have a worse time than I do with it."

"That's because you got all those shrink coping skills and stuff." Callie said.

"Whatever!" Farah laughed.

Liv was dancing around in a circle. She looked like she was having the time of her life. She waved at Adam across the room and he blew her a kiss. They were in a great space. Liv spun around and snapped her fingers. She leaned further into their little circle of friends.

"Speak of the devil and up she jumps." Liv yelled over the music.

Farah and Callie turned and Riley was coming in the door. She wasn't alone. Kane was with her. Farah's mouth dropped. She nearly tripped getting to the doorway.

"Are you serious? Why would you bring him here?" Farah yelled at Riley.

Kane spoke first. "Bryann is my cousin. She does need to know who her birth family is. Not just Riley."

"Wow Kane! Really? And you chose today to do this? Any other day in the year the two of you could have met with Bryann but you chose today." Farah turned her head to see where Greg was sitting. He had not turned around to see Kane yet. "You know what Riley… people warned me about you. They said that you were a troublemaker who loves to live in destruction. I should have listened. You are a sociopath. I let my desire to build a family for Bryann cloud my professional judgment. You disgust me. I'm so done with you."

Riley opened her mouth. "Farah, Kane is not here to cause trouble and if I would have known you'd be this upset I would not have invited him. You have to believe that."

Farah rolled her eyes and walked away from them. She needed to go update Greg on everything. Surprisingly he was fine. He was locked into a stare with Jessica and they both looked happy. Farah was happy for him.

Suddenly, there was a ruckus from across the room. Riley was standing at the doorway lunging at someone and Kane was holding her arms. There was a crowd of adults around them so Farah could not see exactly what was happening. Greg jumped up from the table and ran over to the doorway. The music was still blaring. "Shake it off" rang over everyone's head.

When Farah got to the crowd and pushed through she saw Kendall…with his wife. "Oh God!"

Riley was screaming but it was still hard to hear her over the music. "How dare you bring her here!"

It was unclear if Riley was trying to get ahold of Kendall or his wife. But it was clear that if Kane lost his grip on her there was going to be bloodshed. Farah looked out over the room and saw Bryann scurrying out the back door of the dance hall. "Bryann!" she yelled and ran after her. By the time Farah made her way through the crowd of teenagers on the dance floor, Bryann was gone. She saw a bright red Nissan Altima pulling out of the parking lot. Farah hung her head in defeat.

She moved back into the party room. Kendall and Riley were still shouting at each other. His wife stood silently beside him. The difference between the two women was way more than day and night. It was like day and the apocalypse. Riley was a C4 packed bomb and Kendall's wife was firecracker with a wet wick.

Callie cleared the crowd from around the couple and then moved all of them out into the hallway. Kendall's wife still had not said a word. It was odd.

Liv leaned over to Farah, "Maybe she's sedated. I know I would be."

Farah smiled because there was a time when Liv stayed sedated. But today she seemed to be a social drinker. It's amazing how someone without the alcoholic gene can just decide to drink less and do it. What was a ten-year battle for Farah was just a matter of choice for her friend, Liv.

Kendall's voice bellowed. "Why didn't you tell me about this party. You claim to want to build a family for this little girl but you only want things on your terms Riley."

Kane whispered in Riley's ear, "I hate to say I told you so but…"

"Shut up!" Riley screamed at Kane. "I didn't tell you because I knew you were going to bring her." Riley pointed her finger as if it had a blade at the end.

Meanwhile, Kendall's wife stood there with glossed over eyes and a closed mouth with just a hint of an upward turn. Liv was probably right. His wife looked like she was sedated.

Riley continued. "Look at her. She's too weak to even speak…"

Kendall's wife opened her mouth and words quietly flowed out with what seemed to be a lot of effort. "Why do I need to speak? I've been listening to you for almost twenty years now, Riley."

"No she did not say my name!" Riley took off toward Kendall's wife but Kane still had her arms so her feet slipped out from beneath her. She turned to Farah. "And you! You sneaky bitch! You should have told me."

Farah smiled. This was her opportunity. She spoke quietly trying to mock Kendall's wife, but not in jest. Farah spoke in the sweetest voice possible. "Riley, Kendall is not here to cause trouble and if I would have known you'd be this upset I would not have invited him. You have to believe that."

Callie and Liv both giggled. Even Kane had to laugh at that one. It was true. Farah had thrown Riley's words right back at her within 15 minutes and it felt good to do it.

Riley lashed out at Farah again. "That's why your husband is in there with his girlfriend."

Farah was fully composed, "Oh sweetie. That's not my husband. That's my EX husband and his wonderful new girlfriend. You should probably be more concerned with your boyfriend being here with his wife. Don't you think?" Farah had an annoying pep in her voice that raised an octave at the end.

A hearty laugh escaped Callie's lips. "That was pretty good, Doc." She said to her friend.

Riley turned around and glared at Callie. Her eyes were filled with fire. Farah got nervous. *"Oh no!"* she thought. *"Not now. Not now. "*

Before Farah could stop Riley from speaking she spewed from her lips. It was as if Farah could actually see the letters coming from Riley's mouth. "What are you laughing at Callista? You have enough to worry about your relationship."

"My relationship is just fine. Thank you. I think you have enough on your plate to be worrying about me and Acer." Callie said with a powerful grin.

Farah stood paralyzed, unable to even blink. She braced herself. Riley shrugged. "You're right. I was done with Acer months ago?"

Callie's eyes opened wide. "What is that supposed to mean?"

"Ask your bestie." Riley mocked.

"Farah?" Callie turned to her friend. "What is she talking about?"

Farah could not open her mouth. Callie saw her face and turned screaming toward the dance floor. "ACER GOODWYN!"

Farah turned toward Riley. "You are toxic. It's no wonder you are all alone."

"The last time I checked. You seem to be alone too." Riley touted.

Farah rolled her eyes and went after Callie. By the time she got to the opposite corner of this boxing ring disguised as a sweet sixteen party, Callie was lighting into Acer and he was desperately trying to explain.

"But...but.."

"But what? But what!" Callie yelled.

"But it was before you."

"You should have told me." Callie bellowed.

Farah thought to herself. *"Just say she's right."*

"You are 100% right." Acer said.

That diffused Callie somewhat. Farah suggested that they go somewhere and talk in private. She let them know that Bryann had taken off in the car with someone and she was unsure if she'd come back to even cut the cake.

"Did she take her meds?" Callie asked.

"She said she did, but now I'm not sure." Farah said.

"Okay well, after I dump him I'll be back to look for her." She turned to Acer. "Let's go…NOOOOOW!"

Acer followed behind Callie like a little puppy. He did love her and he had been so afraid that she would find out about Riley. Greg was right. He had been saying from the beginning that Riley was destructive. Farah thought they had a clear understanding after their talk. Apparently not.

About that time Greg approached Farah. "You happy now?"

"What? Huh?" She looked up at her ex-husband.

"Are you happy now? I told you…"

"I know. I know Greg. Listen…Bryann left here nearly an hour ago. She's in a red Nissan and I have no idea who is driving.

"Is she taking her meds?" he asked.

"OH MY GOD! Everyone keeps asking me that. YES! YES! YES! She said she's taking her meds." Farah shouted.

"But you don't know if she is. Too busy running behind your boyfriend I guess."

"What? Greg, please."

"Where is my daughter?" Greg asked.

Kendall walked up behind them. "Yes where is my daughter?"

Greg turned in complete disbelief. Kendall's chest was swollen full of air and Greg's matched his. Before Farah could say anything Greg punched Kendall right in his face.

Kendall fell to the ground. His wife stood in the corner with a bigger smile on her face. Clearly, her husband getting knocked to the ground delighted her.

Kendall sprung from the floor and wrestled Greg to the ground. At this point the crowd…even the kids could see what was happening. The DJ stopped playing. Riley sat at her table in roaring laughter. Adam ran over to help pull them apart but the two men were locked together like they had horns on top of their heads.

Parents started getting their things and leaving with their children. Farah ran to the door. "Please. Please don't leave."

Several moms just shook their heads and left he building. The one who remained only wanted to watch the reality TV show happening before their eyes. And to top it all off, the birthday girl was missing.

Farah walked toward the back door. She passed the bar and looked at the appealing bottles. She thought for a moment and kept walking out to the back parking lot. Finally she sat on the steps and cried.

She did not know what else to do. Then she closed her eyes but tears still fell out of them onto the ground below her. "Dear God, she whimpered. It's Farah. Help me."

A voice behind her bellowed, "Amen."

It was Kane. He sat down beside her and didn't say a word. He just held her. He did not try to comfort her. She lifted her face towards his and tried to kiss him.

He pulled back. "No! That's not going to make you feel better."

"Yes it is. It is." She sniffled.

"It's not. Farah, why did you just pray?" he asked.

"Because I need God."

"Do you believe in God now?" he asked.

She shrugged. "I guess."

"You guess?"

"I do. I've been trying to talk to him but it doesn't feel right."

"Maybe because he doesn't know you. Would you like to know Jesus?"

Farah looked at him. Tears streamed from her eyes. She thought of all the things that had happened in her life. She mumbled. "He doesn't love me."

"He does. He loves all of us." Kane said.

Farah got angry. "Does it look like he loves me? Look at this mess! Greg is fighting. Callie is going to kill Riley. And who the heck knows where my daughter is?"

"God does." Kane smiled.

"Why did you change?" She asked.

"Because I needed him."

"I need him." Farah said.

"Well tell him. Tell him what you feel. Just talk to him and know he hears you."

Farah was crying so much that a tiny puddle had formed on the floor beneath her. She sniffed. She was not sure if what Kane was saying was true but it was worth a try. Everyone she had ever known to be religious was either mean or crazy. Her Aunt Janice was both.

Farah bowed her head and stared into the water beneath her feet. "God. Please help me. Forgive me for all the things I've done wrong. I'm sorry. I wish I could have been a better person but I don't know how. Can you help me? Can you change me the way you changed Kane?"

Kane squeezed her hand.

"And God can you help me find my daughter. Please keep her safe until I can find her and take her to a rehab center. Please don't let the driver be high too. Please do something with all that mess inside the party. I can't do it God. I can't do it. You have to do something for me. For once, can you do something for me?"

Then Farah thought about what she had said. "I'm sorry God. You have done a lot for me. You got me through medical school. You brought me great friends. You brought me my daughter. And God you kept me alive in that car when my mom died. I'm sorry. Help me God. Change me God."

"In Jesus name," Kane concluded. "In Jesus name."

As soon as Farah lifted her head she heard giggles. Four girls piled out of the Nissan Altima. Bryann was the last one out. She had a bouquet of roses in her arms.

"Mom? What's wrong?"

Farah wiped her nose. "I was worried about you honey. Where did you go?" Farah smiled when she saw all of the girls with Bryann. She had not been with a boy at all. She was not drunk or high or naked.

"I wanted to get some flowers. Come inside I have a surprise."

"Great party Mrs. Goodwyn!" One of the girls shouted as she passed by.

Kane looked at Farah. "You belong to Jesus now. Are you ready to go back in?"

Farah nodded. "But I don't feel different."

"You will." Kane said. "You will."

When they arrived back inside Farah looked around the room. Greg and Kendall were at a table in the corner with their arms around each other's shoulders. Both of them looked beat to the pulp but they were in hysterical laughter. Kendall's wife and Jessica seemed to be having a great conversation. Acer and Callie were holding hands at their table. Though Callie was giving Riley dirty looks, there seemed to be no bloodshed. The room was still full. It was hard to tell that anyone had left the party at all. The DJ was playing music again and the kids were dancing and laughing.

Farah looked at Kane in complete surprise. "What happened in here?" She was puzzled.

"You prayed. God happened."

"But…I don't understand." Farah's face was startled.

"You won't always understand. Just say thank you."

She looked up at the ceiling at the purple and pink butterfly lighting. "Thank you.." she said with a bit of question in her voice.

Bryann interrupted her thought. She watched her beautiful daughter take the stage and grab the microphone. "Hi everyone. Thank you for coming to my party."

The noise in the room started to fade and the music was turned down to provide background to her words. "Some of you know me really well", she said. "Some of you…thank goodness…have met me recently." Those who knew her laughed at her self-deprecating humor.

"I'd like to thank my parents and family for throwing me the most memorable bash of my life. I've got to tell you guys. I really thought there would be a whole lot of drama. My family has been through a tough time lately." She looked at Farah and Greg. "But this was such a fun time and I'm happy to report no drama."

There were a few mumbles in the room. Farah looked at Kane. "She…she doesn't know." Farah's mouth was open a bit in disbelief.

"She didn't see it," he said. "She must have left before she knew what was happening."

"Thank you God." Farah said with a smile.

Kane smiled too.

Bryann continued her speech. "I'd like to call my mom and dad to the stage…my real mom and dad."

Farah and Greg stood and walked to the stage. Surprisingly, neither Kendall nor Riley moved.

Kendall shouted out to Greg. "We got that straightened out."

The crowed laughed and Bryann had a confused look on her face. "Okkkaayyy…" she continued. "And you guys…that's my birth father. Kendall and umm…Mrs. Kendall can you come up here?"

"Lorraine," Kendall shouted. "Her name is Lorraine."

"Mrs. Lorraine, please come, too."

Lorraine got up from the table with a smile. From the stage, Farah could see Riley cringe in her seat. Farah said another quick silent prayer. She saw Kane in the back corner smiling with his hands locked together like he was still praying. But he kept eye contact with her and nodded his head. She smiled at him.

"And ladies and gentlemen, please meet the one of the coolest old women I have ever met. She is responsible for me being here today…I mean alive. Meet my birthmother. Riley."

Riley stood to her feet with great pride. There were only a few claps in the room. Bryann had a puzzled look on her face. "Come on. It's okay. You can give her a round of applause." More applause came at Bryann's request.

When Riley got on stage, Farah walked over and gave her a hug. Then the room erupted in applause and tears. Bryann was smiling bright enough to light the room on her own.

Bryann stood on stage with all of her "parents". She was beaming with pride and Farah was so grateful. Bryann had been taking her medication and she was doing well. Farah was so thankful. She looked at Riley and they embraced again smiling at each other.

"Oh wait…I almost forgot. Auntie Liv and Uncle Adam can you guys come up here too?"

Liv acted shocked. She clutched her pearls in jest. She and Adam kissed and headed to the stage. They stood next to Greg.

Bryann cleared her throat and her voice started to break. "Last, but certainly not least. I want everyone to meet my godparents. My Uncle Acer is my Dad's real brother, but also my godfather."

Acer leaned into Callie, "I told you that was silly. Even she knows it's silly."

Callie elbowed him in the side and shushed him.

"And my Aunt Callie, who used to be the coolest old woman I knew."

Callie stopped in her tracks and put her hands on her hips. Riley dawned a big smile.

Bryann laughed. "But now I realize that she's not as quite as old as I thought…"

"Oh! Okay." Callie smiled and made her way to the stage with Acer. She sneered at Riley, who winked at Acer, as they went by.

Farah frowned at both of them.

"What?" Callie shrugged.

"It's her," Riley whispered. "She never liked me."

Farah whispered back through smiling teeth. "Because you are both just alike."

They all locked arms in big hug around Bryann who announced. "This is my family." The room erupted in applause and there was not a dry eye in the place. Even Kane was in the back of the room crying. Jessica sat at the table wiping her eyes with a tissue.

Farah whispered up to Greg, "Should we have Jessica come up here too."

Greg smiled at Farah…"Uh let's hold off on that a while." He nodded to the back of the room. "What about Kane?"

Farah grinned at him. "Ditto." They laughed together.

Farah stood on stage under the bright lights looking out into the sea of people and butterflies in the room. She exhaled. She had not made a family out of this bunch and she realized she could not do it alone. But somehow, some way…they managed to not kill each other in the process of celebrating her daughter. And in the words of Bryann, "That's kind of a big deal."

As Bryann's family started to file off the stage the DJ played the song "We are family" and everyone began to dance.

Then Acer took the microphone. "One more moment please. Just one more moment and we can get the party started back up again."

Greg and Farah looked at each other. Liv leaned back to look at Farah and she shrugged. Callie looked as if she had seen a ghost.

"I know his is my niece-slash-goddaughter's birthday party and I don't want to steal the show but I can't let another moment pass. This is the time."

Greg and Adam mumbled something but Farah could not hear them. The family was still on stage but backed up to give Acer some room.

The room started to rumble. Farah saw Bryann take a deep breath like she was bracing herself for something bad to happen. Acer looked over at Bryann. "Relax…I'm just going to give you your gift."

"Now?" Bryann asked her uncle.

"Yep," He said.

"Okay." Bryann shrugged her shoulders.

"Callista Piper." Acer waved his hand for Callie to come help him. "Everybody, Callie and I have a lot in common. We don't believe in love. She doesn't and I don't. We think love is a made up emotion." He looked at Callie with mist in his eyes. "But I do believe in us" he said as he went down on one knee.

Bryann jumped up and down clapping her hands hysterically. The entire place went crazy in applause and whistles.

"Detective Callista Piper, will you marry me?"

Callie looked at Acer with such anger in her face. She was embarrassed. She folded her arms and he braced himself. Then Callie looked over at Riley and stuck out her tongue. "YES!" She giggled. "Yes I will!!"

Bryann was elated. She wanted her godparents to be married for so long. She grabbed the microphone. "So my parents are divorced but my godparents are getting married. Yay!!" She hugged Callie and Acer.

Farah fell back against the wall. She looked over to the right of the stage where Kane had made his way to the front. They locked eyes. Callie…who hated God for leaving her alone was getting married. And she was marrying someone who had been in her life for many years.

Adam and Liv embraced and kissed each other. "Honey, " Adam said. "I found out that Dylan owns that company."

"You did?" Liv said and pulled back from him. "Yep. The deal is off. We'll have to find some other way to spend time together." He smiled.

"Oh thank you. Thank you." Liv squealed.

"You could have told me," Adam whispered.

Liv just looked up at her husband and melted into his arms. Greg walked off stage and over to Jessica to embrace. Kane came up on the stage and spun Farah around in the air. "Look at God!" he said.

They stood there in embrace. Farah looked over Kane's shoulder and saw Riley standing alone on stage. She had an anger that was fueled with sadness. Farah nodded to Kane to grab her.

"Come here troublemaker." He said and grabbed his cousin.

She pushed them both away. Riley glared down at Kendall and Lorraine. "Look at them. He makes me so sick. They might as well kiss that marriage goodbye."

Farah shook her head. "Oh Riley will you ever learn?"

Riley twister her head toward Farah and sucked her teeth. "Will you?"

Farah folded her hands together and looked up. She looked back at Riley. "I think I already have."

Connect with Kamryn Adams on Social media
Facebook.com/kamrynadams
Twitter.com/kamrynadams
Instragram.com/kamrynadams
Pintrest.com/kamrynpins
Kamrynadams.blogspot.com

Email: Kamryn @KamrynAdams.com

To receive personal coaching from Kamryn

http://myalliancelife.com